Cameron's Control

An Enthrall Novella

Vanessa Fewings

Cameron's Control
Copyright © 2015 Vanessa Fewings

This story is a work of fiction. References to real people, events, establishments, organizations, or locales are intended only to provide a sense of authenticity and are used fictitiously. All other characters, and all incidents and dialogue are drawn from the author's imagination and are not to be construed as real.

Cover design by VMK
Cover photo is by Alexxxey from Shutterstock

Book formatted and edited by Louise Bohmer:
http://www.louisebohmer.com/site/freelance/

Paperback ISBN: 978-0-9912046-5-6
Ebook ISBN: 978-0-9912046-3-2

DEDICATION

To all my readers, thank you for sharing in this journey.

There are fires, vast and endless, that burn in me for you, and I will carry them until you are ready to walk through the flames of me.

William C. Hannan

CHAPTER 1

OBSESSION.

Only now did I understand its true torment.

I'd personally become acquainted with the misery of an impossible conquest.

These endless laps in this ice-cold ocean failed to provide my usual clarity, because all thoughts led back to *her*.

Mia Lauren.

She'd bypassed my defenses. I both loved and cursed her existence for shaking the foundation of my BDSM empire that I rule with a firm and steady hand. My ability to master every moment and everyone around me had been compromised.

The ocean swelled and lifted me, carrying me out farther.

Powering on, slicing through with each breaststroke, my Malibu beach house grew ever more distant. This current called for a certain focus. A practiced discipline. A precise breath control.

Mia.

Back in my head, like a forbidden temptation.

Yet she remained innocent in all this. Having seduced her into our world and delivered her to my best friend and business partner Richard Booth, I truly believed I'd implemented my usual genius. I'd presented her as the ultimate prize.

The plan had been simple enough: find a compatible candidate, study the subject, methodically analyze her every behavior, influence her motivations and manipulate them to dovetail my own, place her under a psychological microscope until her every action could be predicted and my desired outcome guaranteed.

Richard's life had hung in the balance due to his reckless daredevil stunts that included climbing skyscrapers in order to leap off them, and when that no longer got his rocks off, diving into shark infested waters for fun.

I had to ground the bastard.

Provide a distraction. The love of a woman.

Pure. Innocent. Malleable.

A stunning twenty-one-year-old—the perfect prescription.

I'd effortlessly drawn upon my critical ability to comprehend the psyche of our subject, the sweet and innocent Mia Lauren, who was presented as ideal. I'd chosen her from a slew of potentials and plucked her out of the mundane. She held a timidity that was easily enhanced by her ravishing beauty, and a femininity that left men swooning around her. A flawless representation of the sacred feminine.

Her desire to please was a perfect trait for a submissive.

Harsh, perhaps, but the alternative for Richard was unimaginable. He was going to fucking kill himself.

The objective to find the right applicant had gone...swimmingly. Right up until the point *I'd* fallen for her. All I had to do was train her. Break her. Prime her. Ready her.

Tame her.

But she'd trapped me instead.

My once ironclad will was tossed into disarray.

I'd broken the one true rule and fallen for the submissive I was training for someone else.

Fucking unprofessional.

I was fourteen years older than her, yet her feistiness threw me off guard. Her relentless strength, her presence, stirred a primal desire to possess her.

I had to get a grip.

Pushing harder, I fought the rolling waves coming at me.

If I kept this pace up, my energy would fade several miles out and, if caught in a riptide, I'd be screwed. When that realization hit me, I began the swim back to shore.

"Master," her tone breeched my defenses. *"I am yours."* Her words reached me like no other submissive before her.

And like the idiot I was, I'd insisted on delving deeper into her mind, exploring this young woman from a troubled past to better understand my own feelings, try to comprehend why her.

If I wasn't going to destroy my closest friend Richard by stealing her away, I'd have to put this behind me. And fast.

I hoped I'd survive her not becoming mine. A raw truth that stabbed me with the consequences of my actions.

My escape plan to the other side of the world had been sabotaged. My newly fueled jet had been scheduled for takeoff from Santa Monica Airport a few hours ago. My destination, France.

My plane didn't leave the runway. Paris had been derailed by the remarkable circumstances of my reunion with Henry, my older brother. My guilt and pain over what I once believed I'd put Henry through dissipated. His perspective ironically clashed with mine. I'd believed I'd destroyed him back in Afghanistan during a debriefing that had gone terribly wrong.

This morning, Henry had convinced me just how wrong I'd been. After too many years between us ruined by misunderstandings and painful mistruths, we'd spent precious time reuniting. This had been due to Mia's meddling in my personal affairs. Henry was back in my life again. My reclusive older brother, whose war torn scars were the kind reflected in his eyes. The consequences of Mia's visit with Henry had ensured a family's reconciliation and old wounds healed. Yet another life Mia had saved and I'd scolded her for it.

My arrogance once again served as a reminder I didn't deserve her.

I tried to think of anything but her...

My mind filled in the abyss of loss, projecting the vision of a haunting beauty vacillating beneath the morning sun.

Blinking off droplets to see better, my feet found the sand and I waded toward the beach.

Waves crashed around me as I wiped ocean from my eyes.

Mia ran toward me, splashing through the water.

My gaze swept the sand, searching for Richard and questioning why he'd brought her here. To soothe? Taunt? He was like a brother to me, but he was infuriating when it came to matters of the heart.

Mia came closer, standing waist deep in water, breathless. Her blonde locks windswept, her face flushed, and her blue eyes full of hope.

Back at Enthrall, one of my dominatrixes had told me Mia reminded her of a painting by William-Adolphe Bouguereau; an impossible beauty. I'd prided myself on such a remarkable find and not once suspected I too would become enraptured.

Had an argument with Richard sent her back to where it began? This condo, her once safe refuge.

"Richard?" I broke my gaze from hers.

"He doesn't want me anymore."

Her words blurred the lines of possibilities.

Something about her failing as his submissive, something about him sending her away. Something about them being over.

The truth spilled, emphasizing my inability to take Mia where she'd needed to go. My attempt to tame her was unsuccessful. Her feistiness became an unpredictable complication. I'd fallen short of my objective.

"I disagree," I said. "You just require the appropriate handling." That made me grin.

She scrunched up her dress as though her drenched hem could be undone.

Bewitching.

"You're here?" she said. "Not France?"

That diamond bracelet was back on her wrist. The delicate piece I'd placed there way back when I'd allowed myself the luxury of loving that which I couldn't have.

She raised her hand. "What's engraved on it?"

Had Richard really let her go?

I failed to understand how anyone would ever willingly let Mia go without a fight.

"The jeweler told Richard there's writing on it. Only he didn't tell me what."

An engraving naked to the human eye.

My thoughts bounced back to Richard's latest text. Vague words about what I deserved, that happiness was my right too, and I had to trust him and follow through on his wishes.

Surely he'd realize his mistake and come back for her? My focus settled on the horizon.

"Please tell me," she said.

I feigned nonchalance. "It says 'I will always love you.'"

A sob caught in her throat and she teetered forwards.

It was heart-wrenching to see her like this.

"Say it. Say the words."

"I just did, Mia."

"No, say it to me like you're not reading it off my bracelet."

Bury these feelings. You have no right to her.

"Technically it's my bracelet." Another shrug. "As it's on your wrist."

She stomped her foot and went under, disappearing.

Nothing mattered.

Only her.

Sweeping her up in my arms, scooping her out of the water, I pulled her into my chest and clutched her to me, overwhelmed with how good it felt to be this close again. Wading toward land with her in my arms, all I wanted was her to be safe.

All I needed was to see her happy.

"That's you saving me again." She nuzzled into my chest.

My body ached with need.

These games were over. This power play between two friends had done its worst to an innocent girl and I refused to see the woman I loved in any more distress.

I bent my head and kissed her.

"You need a girlfriend who's also your sub," she said.

"I quite agree. However, I have one stipulation, Mia."

Her body stiffened in my arms.

"You must agree to a permanent contract."

"Forever?"

I smirked. "That's what permanent means, yes."

She gave that sweet, petulant pout I'd come to adore.

Her feistiness sparked this temptation, this need to own her beyond what she knew was possible.

"Say yes," I demanded.

"Yes, please. When?"

"Right now. If you fail to call me sir."

She looked up at me. "Sir."

5

The promise of being inside her returned, bringing her the kind of pleasure she deserved. *Needed.*

Grabbing her hand, I pulled her back toward the condo. "Much better, Ms. Lauren."

"It's New Year's Eve."

I stared down at her. "A new life."

Her expression was a mixture of wonder and surrender, and she seemed too drenched in love to care about her dress.

I squeezed her hand. "Mia Lauren."

"Yes?"

"I love you so much. I've always loved you. From the moment I laid eyes on you. And I always will. You're everything I could've dreamed of and more."

She leaned against me. "I love you, Cameron Cole."

My kiss was harsh, lavishing affection, a dark prelude to all I was about to do to her. I broke away. "My sweet, sweet, Mia. You are enthralling."

Through the glass sliding door we hurried and I spun around and closed the blinds.

"Mia," I commanded, "out of those clothes."

Her expression turned to wonder as her fingers worked the straps, fumbling nervously.

I stepped forward. "Remember what I told you?"

Captivation swept over her. "If I was yours?"

In London, owning her had seemed so out of reach.

"Mia, I told you I'd possess you beyond all understanding."

"I remember."

"Time to show you what I meant."

CHAPTER 2

I EXHIBITED THE kind of patience that would have impressed a Tibetan Monk.

After taking a shower *alone*, needing my thoughts to settle and to regain my self-control, I rejoined Mia in the bathroom.

She showered off the seawater. Her gaze met mine and quickly slipped away, her shyness endearing. She looked ethereal beneath that heavy downpour, her nakedness clouded in a veil of steam.

This self-denial was a punishment in its purist form.

From the way she turned away she too felt this unnerving chemistry between us. We were lightning in a bottle, the freeing of which threatened to change us irrevocably. We'd smash the worlds we'd come from and forge a new one together.

Holding off on touching her, I merely watched and waited, delaying the pleasure of our impending session.

The white bathroom tile, hardwood floors, and luxury tub in the center had all been picked out personally by me when I'd decorated this place for her way back when she had no idea I owned this condo. Other than Richard, no one else knew Mia was here. We were assured privacy for as long as we wanted it.

My hands balled into fists as I fought with my conscience. I should do the right thing—refuse her, refuse me, and take her back.

Our love was pure.

My doubt hadn't been about that.

7

I'd refused to go there, imagine an *us*. There rose a lingering concern she'd not survive a relationship with a man like me: controlling, dominating, and with an acquired taste for the dark arts.

My heart screamed my thoughts into silence.

I gestured for her and she turned off the faucet.

After drying Mia with a plush towel, I ordered her to proceed naked into the bedroom. She knelt and leisurely crawled beside me along the hallway, her movement showcasing the elegance of a tamed submissive.

The vision of her subservience, the way the afternoon light flooded in from the bay windows and reflected off her pale skin, her feminine movement of freely giving herself over to me, all took my breath away.

Within the privacy of the bedroom, she rose to her feet as commanded and held the submissive's pose. She held it beautifully—liberated by her nakedness, the ends of her hair damp from the shower, her eyes averted, her spine straight, her hands held together behind her back. Serene, feminine, the exquisiteness of surrender.

She responded to the tone of my command, which remained severe and all- controlling. This would mark our first session as lovers.

My sub was not just any woman. She was the flower I'd helped blossom from the start, and her continued flourishing would occur by my own hand no less.

The art of masterdom I knew well. I was more than capable of ensuring my submissive's desires were fulfilled on every level, her secret yearnings brought into the light, her needs explored, her fantasies realized, her orgasms given the exploration and longitude they deserved. The art of taking a completely vulnerable sub and guiding her through the scene were beyond any pleasure I'd known. I was no different to any other master, demanding complete satisfaction too from the play.

I ran my hand over Mia's soft flesh, down her back, along her buttocks, pinching and squeezing, priming her tenderness.

This position led her beautifully into the scene, highlighting her physical, emotional, and psychological willingness to proceed. She slipped into subspace effortlessly, her eyes flitting to mine.

The inspection began with the slow steady examination of her breasts, nipples tweaked and pinched and elongated until those pink buds had my approval. Her beautiful body was a pleasure to explore.

"Show me." I gestured.

Mia obediently laid her hands on her labia, easing it apart, nudging her hips forward for me to better see. "Yours, sir."

If it were possible to die from an aching cock, I was close. My balls were tight and full, my chest was heavy with need, and my entire body tingled.

"Did I give permission to speak?"

A flicker of blonde curls as she shook her head. Her flushed cheeks reflected the tension of being so exposed. Her sex enticed me.

Running my hand along her cleft, her arousal wet the tips of my fingers. A surge of emotion swept over me as that delicate clit throbbed beneath my touch.

Mia let out a long sigh.

I stepped back and stared into her blue eyes. "Forgive me. I can't."

This building intensity scrambled my thoughts and made it hard to focus.

Devastation marred her face.

"No, Mia, what I mean is…"

Tears moistened her eyes.

Couldn't do it.

Couldn't take her through an hour long scene and deny myself any longer, deny her. Sweeping her up, I forged ahead toward the dresser and sat her on it, pulling her thighs apart and stepping between them, freeing myself from my pants.

With a yell of need I thrust into her, burying deep, her slickness aiding my strike of power. I grabbed her hair and tugged it back. "I refuse to give you up," I yelled. "I will fight to keep you no matter what."

"Oh, Cameron." Her eyes lit with passion.

Her head fell back and her groans proved her closeness.

This, this was what we both needed right now, me fucking her fiercely, taking her there fast, and with her eyelids lowered, her jaw slack, and her groans of pleasure rising above mine, she proved she needed this too.

Driving her harder, feeling her sex clenching in rhythmic squeezes, I leaned forward and braced my hands against the wall. The sensation of this rising in my cock stole all air from my lungs. My muscles flexed, my body went rigid, and I dominated her every move.

She screamed her orgasm.

Our wildness continued unabated.

Lifting her off the dresser, I spun her round so her back was against my front and I clasped her hands behind her. With her wrists secured tightly in my left hand, I reached around with my right and found her clit and gave it the play it deserved, the pleasure she yearned for, until she pleaded for release.

I leaned back against that dresser and, like a mad man, went with her into this frenzy, bringing her down on me sharply, filling her completely, stretching her, feeling her tautness. Mia's thighs were spread wide over mine, providing continued access to her sex while my fingers strummed their perfect rhythm.

My other hand took possession of her breasts, tweaking her nipples into elongated buds—pert and firm, full of want.

Our fucking grew more frenzied.

As though we didn't believe we were here. During those many nights spent apart, I woke with her name on my tongue and my body rigid and ready to claim her, as though she slept beside me. Where she had always been destined to be.

So many restless nights of missing her.

Wrapping my arm around her waist, I increased our pace and brought her down hard on me, burying deep, and with each thrust deeper still, until her thighs trembled and her breaths were ragged, and her spasms carried her fast toward bliss.

Blood roared through my ears. I was too delirious to care about anything but her, too enraptured with the sound of her cries, her gasps. My fingers brought her over as her head fell back against my chest and she surrendered completely, her sex gripping my firmness, owning me too.

Filling her with warmth, I came hard. All thoughts scattered as time and place dissolved from awareness and all I knew was her.

Mia trembled in my arms.

I rocked into her gently, still buried deep, savoring her small cries as I brought her over again.

And again.

My fingers explored, worshiping every inch of her, wanting nothing more than to soothe with these endless caresses.

Mia was finally mine.

And I gave a silent prayer, promising to dedicate the rest of my life to protecting her and ensuring her happiness.

We changed positions again, refusing to end this fucking. We lay, we stood, and I even took her while standing with Mia's legs wrapped around my waist, until we eventually made it to the bed. Our tussling on the four-poster reflected how much we didn't want to let go.

Hours slipped by…

Collapsing, we dozed off in each other's arms.

A deep sleep of peacefulness.

I awoke to find Mia gone.

I flung my legs over the edge of the bed as a well of panic filled my lungs. I went in search of her. This pit in my gut was too cruel to endure.

And there she was, in her bra and panties, standing in the kitchen, drinking from a tall glass of water.

I'd forgotten how fond of breathing I was.

She had a grip on me I didn't think possible.

"I was bringing you up one." She pointed to the ice-filled glass on the counter.

"You okay?"

"Thirsty." She beamed at me.

Yet she was an unquenchable thirst.

There was no way to tell her of the panic I'd felt waking up to find her gone. My heartbeat settled, and the dryness of my mouth soothed as I drank that water.

We didn't make it to the bedroom.

I carried Mia into the living room and threw her upon the sofa and ripped off her bra and panties and then buried my face between her thighs.

She shuddered against me and I exulted with how quickly she responded to my tongue lavishing affection, flicking the delicate clit, tasting her perfection, her wetness, an unmatched intimacy.

Desire willed me on to take her quick and hard. Indeed, punish her for making me feel this way—

Ruined by her.

It felt like drowning, and I went under willingly, my heart soaring with every second of being close to her again.

I couldn't recall ever coming so many times in such a short space of time. My cock rose minutes after each climax, as though addicted.

With her hand in mine, I led Mia into the bathroom, letting go only long enough to run a bath for her. I guided Mia into it and directed her into the center.

Like the good submissive I'd trained her to be, Mia stood in the half filled tub, allowing me to bathe her. I slid this soap soaked sponge leisurely up and down her spine, languishing over her buttocks, and lower still. Her trembling revealed her response to my touch.

Yes, I'd ravished her in the past, brought a perfect balance of both pleasure and pain to woo her, but what lay ahead was an intensity of belonging to a lover who prided himself on a certain brand of masterdom.

Should my ownership of her become too much, the return of Mia to her old master was still possible. I needed her to know this.

My jaw tightened. "Should you have doubts about me, about us—"

"Don't," she said. "Not now, not after all we've endured to be together. Trust it. Believe it. I do."

"Mia."

"All I need is your love."

Shaking my head, I marveled at her understanding and squeezed the sponge, allowing warm water to trickle over her. "Warm enough?"

"Yes, thank you." She turned and rested her hand against my face. "You?"

My cheek tilted into her palm and rested there. That gentle gesture of hers felt so endearing, so tender. I'd disallowed either of us to share this before, for fear our bond might have grown too intense.

How futile that all seemed now.

The glaring truth had been right there for everyone to see. My heart had brought me to this place and I only hoped Richard would forgive me. This conflict was all-consuming, this nagging doubt a better man would give Mia back to him. Yet I knew no one could love her like me, and the thought of losing her wrenched my heart too fiercely to fight against this.

Mia wouldn't suffer one more second because of a complex friendship between Richard and I. A tenuous fault line that would no doubt heal.

I wouldn't be able to relax until I'd spoken with him. Until I knew he'd forgiven me for this time spent with the most beautiful creature I'd ever seen, or touched, or tasted. Her skin was silk beneath my fingertips, her elegant curves drew my hand like the darkest bewitchment, and her enduring femininity stole my focus.

"Climb in with me," she whispered.

My hands rested around her waist and I shook my head, coming out from this trance.

All I knew was her.

We bathed together.

We were lovesick, spending the day finding new rooms to fuck in, ordering in food so we didn't have to leave the house, and taking long walks on that golden sandy beach hand in hand, sometimes talking, sometimes silent, but always in tune with each other's needs.

I couldn't remember the days before her.

CHAPTER 3

PERCHED MAJESTICALLY above the Sunset Strip rests an exclusive enclave of homes, all of them belonging to the rich and famous. Their coveted panoramic view of twinkling lights born from that sprawling metropolis, and beyond a dramatic vista of a black velvet ocean.

Hollywood's rising starlet Andrea Buckingham lived in one of the largest homes situated on Doheny Drive. The blacked out glass fronted windows ensured privacy from overzealous fans and eager paparazzi with their long lenses of invasion.

For me, hailing from the East Coast, this town had once held an intriguing appeal. Though after a slew of celebrity patients, I'd gained insight into the vacuous world of the film industry and the town had lost its sparkle. Though not for Mia, who sat to my right, all starry eyed by the trail of famous faces wandering into the private party.

Tonight, on New Year's Eve no less, we were gate crashing.

Inside our limousine we'd been shielded from the chill, and I'd asked Leo to turn up the heat so Mia wouldn't feel the cold.

The time from Malibu to here had dissipated effortlessly. I'd been engrossed in Mia and hardly noticed the flashing billboards of the Sunset Strip, and paid little attention to the clubs, restaurants, boutiques, or partying crowds.

We'd spent our first day together mostly wrapped in each other's arms.

Mia reached out and took my hand, gazing at me beneath long lashes, her blue eyes alight with wonder. I drew on my will of steel not to take her again right here in the car, though having her dressed in this elegant shimmering Armani gown, with its hand sewn crystals and delicate gold weaving, influenced my decision.

A few hours ago I'd made a call to my stylist, Sylvia Hudson, and she'd turned up at the beach house with a selection of dresses for Mia to choose from. Sylvia matched Mia's favorite dress with elegant Christian Louboutin shoes.

Sylvia had worked for me long enough to know to bring one of my bespoke black tie suits and these Salvatore Ferragamo shoes.

I'd brought hardly anything to the beach house. I'd not intended on staying for more than a few hours. My path crossing with Mia's felt like a gift.

Her endless show of gratitude was endearing, but now she was part of my life and I insisted she take all this luxury in stride. She was going to have to get used to it and I'd taken her aside during Sylvia's visit and told her this.

That thin strip of rubies now served as her new collar. I'd removed the other one and secured it in the bedroom safe and expedited delivery of this exquisite handmade piece from my Beverly Hills home.

Lincoln, my personal butler, had brought it to Malibu as per my request. I didn't tell Mia she was wearing millions for fear she wouldn't enjoy it.

The choker had once belonged to my Aunt Rose, who'd told me it should be given to *the one*. This piece represented the kind of commitment I was now ready for.

We talked endlessly.

Mia shared her experiences of working in Willem's Art store in North Hollywood. During her early days in the city, there was no way she could have imagined a place like Enthrall. Her stories made me laugh. Like the one about a colorblind artist who Mia always tried to guide when choosing paints for his next masterpiece. She'd even hung his work inside the studio beside the store and supported the young man's clashing concoctions. Her nudging the starving artist toward more pleasing palettes and her effort to sell his pieces to the art loving crowd afforded him to eat at least.

We talked about her future and she questioned me on a career in psychology. A profession she had a natural inclination for.

Every second with her felt right. No one came close to captivating me like she did. Her soft southern lilt, those innocent words flowing unabashedly, those plump, full lips that were now mine to kiss.

It was hard to grasp that only this morning I'd packed a suitcase for Paris. It made me happy to think I'd be taking Mia on my next trip to France. I couldn't wait to show her the rest of Europe.

The impossible unraveled in what felt like another life, proving once again this sense of control was a ruse.

"How's Henry?" she asked.

"Fine. He's hanging out at the Venice Beach house. I gave him some space."

"Did you surf?"

"Not yet. We bought boards though. We just sat and talked." It had felt as though no time had slipped between us.

Our past was a mixture of a shared childhood and later, when duty called, Henry had joined the military and I'd attended Harvard. That final deployment had seen Henry come undone, his capture and subsequent torture in an Afghanistan encampment had almost destroyed him. I'd taken him the rest of the way, or so I'd believed, debriefing him to extract strategic information. The words he'd eventually spew had merely been digits and codes, but central intelligence had connected the dots and subsequently intercepted an attack on our homeland.

Henry had been sent home to recuperate in a psychiatric wing and I'd endured these last few years believing with all my heart I'd been the one to put him there.

Without telling anyone, Mia had visited my brother and leant her own brand of healing. Her sweet innocence was all it took for me to forgive her meddling.

"You found his address in my office?"

"I'm sorry." She looked at me warily. "I couldn't see you sad anymore." She turned her head away. "I'd go visit him again if I knew it would help you both."

"You know that doesn't make any sense, right?" I said, amused. "You can't apologize and then tell me you'd repeat the behavior."

"Behavior," she scolded. "The rift between you and Henry had to end. Anyway, I really like him. He's special. But then again he's a Cole."

"We'll see how he does out of Big Bear."

"I think he was lonely in that cabin."

I reached for her hand. "He knows we're here for him."

Leo navigated the car curbside and parked. He climbed out and opened the door for Mia.

I joined them around the other side. "Don't wait," I told him. "Go get a drink with your family."

"How will you get home, sir?" Leo's gaze swept over the newly arriving guests.

"We'll grab a cab."

He looked uncomfortable. "Please, sir, just text me when you're ready to leave. The boys will be in bed. Wife, too. When you've got two young ones, you'll be in bed by eight, too." He laughed.

This ex-marine was a hard man to negotiate with. I offered a nod of thanks and took Mia's hand and led her toward the door.

"Who do we know here?" she asked.

"No one."

She threw me a look of surprise.

I gave a shrug. "Other than Richard."

She tried to pull her hand from mine, but I held it firmly and nodded to the security guard on the way in.

"Cameron?" she whispered nervously.

I beamed across the room at a crowd of guests as though I knew them.

That show of confidence was all it took for us to gain entry. That and the bouncer's gaze locked on Mia. It was the distraction we needed to make our way in unhindered.

It wasn't just the bouncer who was enamored. A few guests who'd gathered by the foot of the stairs turned and stared at us, their expressions probably matching my own when I'd first laid eyes on Mia. Of course I'd seen her in a photograph before I'd met her, but nothing came close to witnessing this kind of ethereal beauty close up.

Mia didn't like the attention, and her defiance wavered as she nudged back up against me. I withdrew my hand from hers and rested it against the arch of her spine.

This primal need to protect her sunk deep into my bones and made me question coming here.

My eyes scanned the crowd for Richard.

We were hit by rock music and the sound of laughter. I spotted a familiar face—that of musician Magnus Anderson. A well-worn guitarist from the band of the moment 'Bound.' He sipped on a tall glass of iced-water. Magnus swallowed hard when a waiter offered him a glass of champagne. He declined it unconvincingly. This was no place for a man on the brink of relapsing.

The old me would have tactfully gone in for the rescue, but Mia was my priority now and so was Richard, so I led her through the foyer and onward into the thick of the party.

The open plan design was perfect for entertaining and hosting hundreds, the vast expanse leading to an impressive room displaying a modernity of light wood and plush pastel colored furniture. That antique chest made a nice touch.

The lavishly decorated living room swallowed us up and I went ahead and reached back for her hand to guide our way to a quiet corner, easing through the exuberant well-dressed men and women. We received respectful nods here and there from the other guests.

Mia's stare flitted over the many faces. Her body stiffened in my arms. I deserved her mistrust after the many times I'd maneuvered her into the place I'd decided was best for everyone. My imperious nature did its worst, and all in the name of love.

She looked so fragile as her gaze searched mine. Doubt for what tonight might bring was etched on her face.

A heart wrenching look of vulnerability.

CHAPTER 4

"MIA, YOU BELONG to me." I planted a kiss to her forehead.

"You just want to make sure Richard's okay?"

"Yes."

She relaxed a little.

"Oh sweetheart." I wanted to ease her angst. "I need you to trust me."

My hug served as reassurance and I caressed her back with affection. Her arms reached beneath my jacket and around my waist. It really did seem like the world had slipped away, if only for a few seconds.

The décor leant an over refined tone. Our host Andrea Buckingham was from the Midwest, and her humble upbringing would mean she wouldn't know the difference between a painting by Sarah Lucas or a sculpture by Damien Hirst, yet from her collection you'd have thought she was an art fanatic. Andrea had evidently handed over her credit card and told the designer to do his worst.

And he had.

One portrait would have blended in well with the cream walls, but this mismatched selection tipped her hand that she yearned to fit in. Some of her guests might have been impressed, but it didn't take me long to extract a profile from Andrea's ornaments and ascertain which ones were those her designer had picked out from trendy overpriced Beverly Hills boutiques.

I'd read about Andrea in a Vanity Fair article, while scanning the pages for more interesting material during a long flight from L.A. to India, six months ago. An annual business trip I'd taken on behalf of Cole Tea. The side of the business I enjoyed.

I turned to check on Mia. She had the ability to stop time in its tracks. Her delicate fingers traced a sculpture, caressing the stone.

"Bo Hadley," I told her.

"You've seen his work before?"

"Afraid so. Took me weeks to recover."

"What do you think this one means?"

"What does it mean to you?"

"Makes me feel unsettled."

"It's meant to evoke an inner confrontation that leads to the deciphering of our inner illusion, or more accurately, delusion that echoes our lives."

Mia looked astounded.

Amused, I pointed to the description on my side of the stand. "In other words a five thousand dollar Hadley."

"I love that you know so much," she said wistfully.

A young couple gave Mia a snarky glare.

I turned away from them after making a quick decision not to verbally eviscerate the couple for their rudeness, preferring to fill my gaze with Mia. Even though she'd caught their arrogance, she hadn't reacted, merely looked up at me with those forgiving eyes.

With her, my mind ceased its endless analyzing, its reckless foray into deciphering human codes during each and every interaction, my thoughts spiraling in demand for answers.

Mia was the only answer I needed.

My pathway to peace.

Still, I was up for some entertainment to repay that couple's rudeness, their snide whispers hinting at their self-absorbed lives.

I threw a smile their way. "This piece reminds me of Freud's theory on art. What was it that Freud thought about artists again?"

Mia looked thoughtful. "Freud believed artists are avant garde psychologists." Her gaze drifted over the sculpture. "And artists understand the laws which activate the unconscious. This is how they reveal their knowledge, through their creations, and as such we are exposed to their comprehension of the human condition." She sucked on her bottom lip as though mulling over her own words.

I looked over at the couple. "Okay, wow, gorgeous and smart too."

Their snide expressions were gone.

More stares found us and we were meant to be keeping a low profile. I hurried Mia through the patio doors and out into the landscaped garden. A burst of fresh air and the scent of lavender caught on the breeze.

To the left was a modest swimming pool and a few guests who'd strayed from the house sat around it. To our right was a carp pond into which a small waterfall fell. Beyond the garden was that dramatic view.

I turned away briefly to accept two glasses of champagne offered from the waiter who'd ventured out here. I gave one to Mia.

We were left alone again.

Careful not to spill champagne, I shrugged out of my jacket and rested it over Mia's shoulders. She fell against me and we both stared out over the sprawling vista. Hugging, it felt like all that had gone before no longer hurt—all the trials, all the confusion, all the denials of love melted into the past.

This, this was different.

A splash pulled our attention toward the pool. A woman had stripped to her underwear and was swimming. She was bathed in blue soft light. Another partygoer removed his clothes and dived in.

"You've got to be kidding me!" Came Richard's incredulous tone.

I beamed back. "Happy New Year to you too, Richard."

He stood a few feet away, holding a bottle of Miller Light. "Thought you'd be at Chrysalis?"

"We chose this instead."

"You know Andrea Buckingham?"

A shake of my head told him I didn't.

He took a swig. "When you asked me what I was doing tonight I didn't think you'd gate crash."

Stepping toward him, I said, "Booth, we haven't spent a New Year's Eve apart in years. It didn't feel right."

Richard patted my back. "Have to admit it didn't." He looked over at Mia. "Pretty dress." His gaze lowered to her shoes and he arched a brow.

"Thank you," she whispered.

He wore ripped jeans and a black J. Crew sweater. His hair was ruffled in his usual *don't give a fuck* style, oozing privilege—the edgy bad boy kind.

It was good to see he was still talking to me.

"I'll get us some hors d'oeuvres," said Mia, removing my jacket and handing it back.

"It's good to see you, Mia," said Richard warmly.

She looked relieved and wrapped her arms around his waist, giving him a big hug. He closed his eyes and leaned into her. "I knew Cameron was visiting the beach house," he told her. "When I dropped you off."

She raised her eyes to look at him.

"It's okay. I need you to know I wouldn't have left you alone otherwise."

Her nod of understanding appeared to comfort him.

This morning now seemed like a lifetime away. Richard and Mia had been on their way to Palm Springs. Only their brief stop at the jewelers to pick up a broken bracelet had changed the course of history.

I'd given it to Mia when I'd trained her and hadn't considered that secret engraving would be discovered. It had been my private declaration of love.

Mia threw me a smile and headed into the house.

Richard stepped up to join me. "Quite the view."

"Richard, I'm so sorry." Words weren't enough.

"Right to the point."

"I fucked up—"

"That bracelet told me everything I needed to know. I suspected you'd fallen hard for her but that proved it beyond all doubt."

"You weren't meant to see what was inscribed on it. No one was."

"Yeah, well, I did."

"You gave her up for me?"

"Nothing's changed, Cam. I'll always love her. Always love you too, you stupid bastard." He took a swig. "That doesn't stop me from wanting to shove my fist through your devilishly handsome face."

"Can't blame you."

"Halfway through her training, I realized how she felt about you. The way she looked at you. And you her. That time I'd snuck into Chrysalis to visit her, the chemistry between you both was off the charts. I hoped it was temporary."

"This was not my intention."

"Promise me you'll take care of her. Don't hurt her, Cam."

"Of course not. Mia's my priority now. Over everything."

His gaze stayed on mine. "She really broke through to you, didn't she?"

Turning to stare through that glass wall, my gaze found Mia nibbling on a bite of food, her expression full of intrigue as she took in the crowd.

God, she was so beautiful.

"You can't tame her, Cam. You know that, right?" he whispered.

"It's fun trying."

"She's so infuriating." Richard followed my line of sight. "Which means she's perfect for you."

I tried to shake off this sense of unease over letting Mia wander around alone.

"She'll be fine," he said.

I gave a nod. "How about you, buddy? How are you doing?"

"Well, wouldn't mind a session with you. Help me dig out this excruciating pain in my heart."

"Richard, I—"

He patted my back. "Have you ever considered I want you happy too? That despite all this confusion, there's actually a good outcome."

"I'll make it up to you."

"Just stop interfering in my life, okay?"

"I really did mean for this to work. For you and Mia…" It hurt to say it.

"You're an arrogant fuck."

I wrapped an arm around his shoulder and he relented and leaned back into me and patted my back firmly.

I'd always been his rock, his guide out of the dark, and here I was causing him pain. But I loved Mia too and protecting her felt primal, a need so raw that being apart felt wrong.

A jolt of uncertainty hit me when I could no longer see her. She'd left the kitchen.

Richard turned and looked out. "Nice house."

"How did you pull off an invite?"

"I was packing my stuff for a jump and debating whether to use a parachute," —he gave a crooked grin – "when I got a call from Andrea Buckingham's personal assistant inviting me here tonight."

"Just like that? Out of the blue?"

"Yeah, we met briefly at a charity event I attended with Hope. We were introduced, but Andrea had an entourage and we didn't talk for long. Didn't think she'd remember me."

"You're very memorable."

His eyebrows rose in that devilish way. "Not sure how they got my number. I was too surprised to ask. Andrea's around here somewhere. I'll introduce you. Tell her you're my plus one so you don't get kicked out." He chuckled. "Might just drink Andrea's beer and take a dip in her pool. No doubt Mia will be in there by the end of the night."

"Where's our host now?"

He shrugged. "Andrea summoned me into her office to talk privately."

"About?"

He grinned. "She wants to research BDSM for a role."

I shook my head, amused. "And how did she find out you're connected to Enthrall?"

"Through a friend of a friend apparently. I'll find out who and ban them."

"What did you tell her?"

"For a woman who's used to getting whatever she wants, I left her shell-shocked. Her assistant Sienna's more my type. Pure sub material."

"Sounds intriguing."

We both stared back at the house.

"Mia will be fine," I said. "She can look after herself."

"Sure."

I took a sip of champagne.

Richard slapped my arm with the back of his hand. "Let's go find her."

"Probably a good idea."

He shook his head in amusement.

We made our way in and nudged through the crowd. I set my glass down on a side table. There were the usual players. The suited up agents and managers. The industry types who even here couldn't be separated from their phones. A landscape of people, the screens of their phones glaring back. Perhaps some were tweeting about being at the party. A few took selfies. Others knocked back drinks and laughed in what looked like the joy of reuniting with old friends.

After a few minutes of scouring the house and not finding Mia, I pulled out my phone and texted her: "Where are you?"

Mia's icon blinked away on my phone. She was writing a text. It stopped. She didn't send it.

Richard peered over my shoulder. "Something wrong?"

With three quick scrolls on my phone, I watched the small red dot beating Mia's location.

Richard rolled his eyes. "Seriously?"

"Don't judge me." I waved the phone. "Comes in handy for moments like this."

The blinking light led us up the staircase and we walked along the hallway following the signal.

A knock at a closed door went unanswered.

I pushed it open and went in, looking around at the sparse furniture of this spare bedroom.

Richard followed me in. "Is that thing right?"

I yanked open the closet door.

And let out the breath I'd been holding since I'd lost her.

"Cameron." Mia's arms were folded across her chest. "Did you stick a bug up my ass when I was sleeping?"

Richard burst out laughing.

"Please be more selective with your choice of words," I scolded, tucking my phone away.

"Then how did you find me?"

I glanced down at her Louboutins. "Why are you in here?"

She really did look harried.

"Mia," I said. "Don't let these people intimidate you."

"I'm not intimidated."

"Good." I glanced over at Richard, who was enjoying this.

"Mia, he's not handing you back to me," he said.

She lowered her gaze. "Where's the bug, Cameron?"

"It's the magic of love. I felt your presence and—"

"Cameron," she snapped.

"Enough of this."

She balled her fists on her hips. "I knew it."

"Mia, trust me, a man in my position—"

"Is it in my shoe?"

I glared at her. "One more word and I'll forbid you to speak for the rest of the evening."

"Seriously Mia," said Richard, "we were looking forward to the hors d'oeuvres you went to get us."

"She who cannot be named is here," Mia blurted. "I needed a moment."

I blinked my reaction.

"McKenzie Carlton?" said Richard.

Mia watched my reaction, which I was currently trying to hide, not least because I'd refused to tell Mia my ex- fiancé's name.

"She must have seen us arrive," said Mia. "Because McKenzie took me aside and told me who she was."

My thoughts ran off trying to work out what Zie was doing in Los Angeles. She'd always moved in these circles but this was uncanny.

"Mia," I said, "you two talked?"

"Yes."

"What about?" asked Richard.

Mia's gaze rested on me.

"Out of there," I snapped. "Now."

She hurried out and stood by my side, her eyes wide and full of caution.

"Let's go find Zie," said Richard, earning himself a glare from me. He shrugged it off. "Or not."

"How about this?" I said, "Let's see the new year in somewhere more…"

"Your place then?" said Richard.

I agreed with a nod.

"I'd like that," said Mia, her cheeks flushed.

Taking her hand firmly in mine, I led her out.

We navigated the guests who sat on the stairs. The party was in full swing. The music grew louder. People were pulling poppers already. Annoying screams of delight sliced through my head. Knowing Zie was here tainted the mood.

The front door was in our sights and we headed toward it.

A tug on the back of my jacket.

That familiar scent of amber wafted; Hermes.

Zie hadn't aged at all and I put that down to an easy life full of privilege and luxury brands that held back the years. Her pale blue chiffon halter dress brought out her feminine curves and emphasized her tall, lean frame. Shiny auburn locks spiraled over naked shoulders. Zie's timeless beauty and razor-sharp cheekbones had always placed her firmly in the spotlight. Her green iris's sparkled with mischief.

The last time we'd been this close we'd been arguing. It had been ugly. Until I met Mia, I'd not loved anyone as much as I'd loved her.

Though my affection for Mia felt different—pure, untainted. The advantage of a new relationship. No cruel history to haunt us.

Zie forced a grin. "Nice to see you too, Cam." She flashed a glance over my shoulder. "Hello again, Mia. I so enjoyed our little chat. Very informative." She gave a crooked pout.

The same one I'd once found endearing, only now it oozed bitchy.

Zie's allure had always been her demure sexuality, her ability to use those overly rouged lips to get whatever she wanted. Whoever she wanted. Whenever she wanted. Zie ran her tongue along her lips to moisten them and rested the tip in the corner of her mouth suggestively. That used to be her way of getting my cock's attention.

Trying to push away thoughts of what this woman was capable of in the bedroom, I peered over her shoulder, pretending to scour the other guests.

I reached back and grabbed Mia's hand to reassure her.

"Richard," said Zie. "You still working at *that* place."

His back stiffened. "Yes, if you're referring to Enthrall." He didn't care who heard. "How's the upper east side? All the happier for you not being there, I imagine."

"We were just leaving," I said.

Zie's eyelids lowered. "Congrats on your engagement."

Yeah, great, my family suspected Mia was now my fiancé, as did the Board of Psychiatry, after that debacle of a hearing to ascertain if I'd mistreated a patient. Only Mia had never been a patient, merely a sub in training. That detail was no one's business.

A polite smile was called for.

"Willow broke the news." Confusion marred Zie's face. "We had coffee last week."

I regretted coming here now.

"Your sister didn't mention seeing me?" she said.

"No, we haven't spoken recently."

"I'd heard on the grapevine that Mia was your submissive, Richard."

"How do you know Andrea?" asked Richard, changing the subject.

"Through Megan Banks. She's Andrea's publicist. Megan and I were in the same sorority."

Zie's days at Yale were legendary, not least because she excelled in her chosen field of art and had been hailed by the Huffington Post as a young Picasso.

There'd been a time when McKenzie's sassy brilliance had set my world on fire. Though now it felt like I was standing in the ash drenched wreckage of what we'd once been.

My gaze drifted toward the door.

"How are your parents?" she asked.

"Fantastic. Yours?"

"Same. That's a pretty choker."

Mia's fingers traced the edge of the rubies and her gaze swept from me and back to Zie.

"You tried to put one of those on me once," said Zie. "Remember? You got a kick out of me refusing to wear it."

"Long time ago," I muttered.

She raised her chin. "Still, I wore it for you in the end. Remember? You were very persuasive. I loved that about you."

"Different choker," I told Mia, wondering what words had been exchanged between them.

Zie glared at Mia.

"Well this has been delightful." I almost sounded convincing. "But if you'll excuse us, we have somewhere to be."

"Cameron." Zie's eyes were full of pain. The same pain I'd caused her way back when I'd realized we weren't right for each other.

I'd bestowed the kind of cruelty undeserving of any woman. The invitations had gone out. The cake design meticulously decided upon. That ivory Vera Wang destined not to be worn.

Those endless nights with Shay and Richard as we drank well into the morning, both of them telling me I'd done the best thing for both of us. And me not sure if I had.

"I'm sorry, what?" I said, rising from hell.

McKenzie looked vulnerable and I wasn't used to seeing it on her.

"I need to talk to you."

"About?"

"It's personal."

"Not a good idea." I gave a thin smile.

Richard nudged my arm. "We're gonna to be late."

I reached up and gave Zie's arm a comforting squeeze. "Another time perhaps?"

Or as I like to put it, *no fucking way.*

Her eyes flicked in response to my touch. "I have an appointment to see you."

"At my office?" I lowered my voice. "I'll book you in with Dr. Laura Raul. She's more—"

"I've been seeing Laura. She believes an appointment with you will bring closure."

Closure. There it was—the most lie infested word known to man.

My jaw tightened from the fact Laura hadn't shared her plan. My junior psychologist was making stupid decisions. I was the radical therapist. Not her. Time working alongside me had backfired.

Zie looked too fragile right now for me to tell her I was going to cancel her appointment. I'd get Patricia, my secretary at the clinic, to call her tomorrow.

"Have a lovely evening," I said and pulled Mia toward the door.

Although I didn't look back, I sensed Zie's eyes on us all the way out. Guilt was right behind me too. All that work I'd done on myself to get over her had now been rendered useless.

Fucking square one.

Leo threw me a wave from across the way.

He'd stubbornly ignored my direct order to go home and spend time with his family. I made a mental note to triple his Christmas bonus.

I joined Richard and Mia in the back of the limo.

Mia got to work on our drinks, pouring champagne into three crystal flutes and then handing them to us.

"Good girl," said Richard, throwing his drink back in one go.

Mia took a long sip. And then another.

Richard and I swapped a wary glance.

"Well that was unexpected," I said dryly.

"She still loves you," whispered Mia.

I winced.

Richard held a crazed smirk. "Happy New Year!"

CHAPTER 5

THEY WERE DRUNK.

Richard and Leo laughed at pretty much everything and it was impossible not to laugh too.

My Beverly Hills home came alive with them here. This twenty-bedroom manor with its stunning if not elaborate furnishings made me look like I believed all this decadence was a good idea. The chandeliers that hung all over the house would have made Liberace blush. All this self-indulgence care of Terrance, my gay designer.

I preferred to hide out in my office or spend time in the modest den.

Though tonight, Richard, Leo, and Mia agreed with my idea to dine alfresco and we settled in the back garden and sipped on chilled Piper-Heidsieck and snacked on grilled scallops wrapped in prosciutto and Lemon-Parsley Gougeres.

It felt good to have such ebullient company.

Out of earshot of the others, I'd teased Mia. "I have plans for you later, Ms. Lauren." And then I'd taken her glass out of her hand and finished off her champagne.

I informed her I had every intention of making tonight memorable. Mia's toes had curled in anticipation.

Dinner was barbequed steak and ribs, which I cooked on the corner grill. We sat around the poolside table to eat. Mia rummaged through the fridge and brought out a few side dishes to compliment the meal, including coleslaw, potato salad, dips and chips, as well as French bread and butter.

Our spontaneous soiree was a refreshing change from the overly stuffy one we'd come from.

I tried to push thoughts of Zie Carlton out of my mind.

Those old doubts circled like vultures waiting to pick at my bones. Yes, life with her wouldn't have been boring, but she was the kind of wild card wise men steered clear of. I had one spontaneous and crazy ass friend in my life, Richard Booth Sheppard, and didn't need another, no matter how stunningly beautiful Zie was or how otherworldly her talent.

Soon after our breakup, I'd returned the pieces she'd painted for me. She'd sold them via Sotheby's. I'd discovered she'd donated the money they'd made to Charlie's, my charity soup kitchen in Santa Monica. Her way of twisting the knife.

Richard arched a brow, peering up from his phone, that boyish grin stuck on his pretty boy face. The kind that had girl's swooning and men crying into their pillow at night when they realized he wasn't bi.

That expression was Richard's way of letting me know he was exchanging texts with Andrea. I imagined she wasn't used to a man with Richard's nonchalance. His hard to get vibe probably sent her into a spiral.

Mia didn't need to know he was being wooed by a celebrity. There'd been enough drama.

After clearing the plates, I dragged four loungers together and placed them to face the pool. The surrounding lush landscaping and majestic trees lining the property provided a safe haven and ensured privacy.

At the stroke of midnight, we all stood with our glasses of champagne in hand and toasted in the New Year, enjoying the neighbor's illegal fireworks.

Cracks and bangs and sizzling lights—

Sparkling colors lit up the night sky and fizzled, only to be replaced by another dramatic display—an endless array of sparks.

Mia and I shared the deepest kiss and her lips were soft and relenting, her tongue surrendering to mine. God I loved her. The impossible had snuck up on me out of nowhere.

In usual Mia fashion, she broke away to hug Richard and then

Leo, making sure in her own indomitable way they weren't made to feel uncomfortable.

More fireworks sparked in the distance, setting the sky ablaze. Birds scattered from branches.

Richard gave a broad smile my way and it felt good to see his playfulness and those kind eyes full of understanding. His refusal to sulk, his devilish attitude toward life, had drawn me to him in the first place.

Our shared love of hedonism had been the catalyst for our club Enthrall in Pacific Palisades, and later Chrysalis, the residential manor in Bel Air that served as an exclusive enclave for the sexually elite. As the kings of hedonism, Richard and I had reigned supreme over the BDSM society. A life any bachelor would envy.

Change lingered in the air.

The sparks were not just in the night sky. I loved seeing the way Mia shied away coyly from my fierce stare, and with that look came proof of her knowing I'd be taking her through her paces soon.

It was hard to take my gaze off her. I yearned to taste her lips again and hold her. These reckless thoughts of locking Mia away and keeping her just for me. This was a mad man's musings, but cage play was all too real in our world and this house had one.

Mia rose and opened another bottle of champagne. She refilled Richard's and Leo's glasses. I turned on the garden heaters to warm us from the chill and set the music to Nina Simone, her soothing voice lulling us with Feeling Good.

Buzzed and heady from the booze, we kicked off our shoes and settled on loungers, snuggling beneath tartan blankets. Rogue fireworks sputtered from someone far off and the sound of cheers rose from behind the wall.

With my phone in hand, I strolled over to the far wall. Taking a few minutes, I shot off a holiday text to Dominic Geddings, my attorney and right hand man. Next came my head of security Shay Gardener, who was also a deadly fencing partner. I also messaged my staff at Enthrall and Chrysalis, the senior dominatrixes Scarlet, Lotte, and Penny, and wished them a great new year.

They all texted back and I laughed at their messages. I really had surrounded myself with the best people.

Scrolling through my contacts, I hit Willow's number.

"I know," she answered warily. "Don't drink and drive."

The music faded in the background, hinting she was moving to a quieter spot.

I chuckled. "Happy New Year, sis."

"Same to you, Cam!"

Despite being twenty-four, I'd always think of Willow as a young girl. It was hard to imagine her all grown up, even with those impressive grades she'd received at Oxford. Her obsession with horses was where her heart lay.

"Where are you?" I said.

"With Rayne."

Her mischievous friend from NYU.

Fucking great.

"Where?" I said.

"Yotel."

Time Square's biggest rooftop terrace on 10th Avenue would be packed, noisy, and too claustrophobic for my taste. I hated she was so far away.

"Be careful," I said.

"Zander's tracking me. Might try to lose him."

"Dad pays him well to keep you safe. Don't make it hard on him. I'm serious, Willow."

"How's Henry?" Her tone was laden with concern.

"I'm keeping an eye on him."

"I texted him, but he didn't get back."

"He's at a SEAL reunion," I said. "On a boat. Probably no reception out on the ocean."

"With Shay?"

"Yes."

"Okay, now I feel better."

"Listen, Willow—

"Oh no, I hate it when you start like that. I survived England, for goodness sake."

I laughed. "Survived one of the most prestigious universities in one of the safest countries."

"Funny."

"I bumped into McKenzie," I said.

"She told you we had lunch?"

"Willow, I'm going to ask you to break off all contact with

her."

The line went quiet.

"Willow?"

"To be honest, she made me uncomfortable."

That sobered me up. "Go on."

"She was asking all sorts of questions about you and Mia. It was awkward."

"I can imagine. What did you tell her?"

"That I'd met Mia."

"You didn't mention…"

"Seeing her naked in your foyer? Of course not."

I caressed my forehead, recalling that evening. The memory would stay with me forever, not least because it was one of the most stunning visions I'd ever seen. Later that night had also been the first time I'd made love to her. She'd presented herself as my submissive, choosing the very evening my family had come to stay. Both my aunt and sister had caught the charade of Mia virtually naked upon her arrival.

My kinky brain had got a kick out of that.

Of course Aunt Rose knew full well she was witnessing a sub's surrender, though she had no idea about Chrysalis. Willow probably put it down to my bachelor ways.

"Honest," said Willow. "I know everything must be kept private. I know the rules."

"McKenzie reached out to you?"

"She told me she was in town and wanted to see me. I didn't see anything wrong with it."

"Thank you for understanding."

"She's still into you."

"She'll get over it."

"I'll delete her number."

"I appreciate that."

"She's not going to go all 'Fatal Attraction' on you, is she?"

"That movie was out before you were born."

"Still."

"Stay safe. Give Zander a break, Willow. It's his new year too."

"I know. I'll not make it hard on him."

"Promise?"

"Promise. Go have fun. You know it's that thing humans do that causes their faces to crinkle all funny."

"You too, Willow." My gaze drifted to the others and I saw Richard pulling a throw over Mia's legs. "I have to go."

"Love you, Cam."

"Love you, Will. Stay safe." I tucked my phone into my pocket and strolled over to rejoin them.

Richard stared down at Mia and when he saw me he said, "She was cold."

"I'm fine, really." Her stare jumped from him to me.

My smile seemed to reassure them both, despite it feeling forced.

Settling on the lounger near Mia's, I focused my scrutiny on Richard. A tilt of his head was his way of telling me everything was fine. Raw empathy raced through my veins and that dreadful guilt returned.

"I like seeing you happy, Cole." His arched brows proved his sincerity.

I gave him that *happiness always has a price* look we so often shared, our friendship so deep words were not needed.

The conversation ebbed and flowed from politics to the financial markets, of which Richard was an expert. Leo shared stories from his time as a marine and he really did have a captive audience. He was more my people than my family.

Richard and Leo verbally sparred over football, though I was only half listening. I was too full of love to really care about the merits of changing the colors of an NFL team's uniform.

Ten minutes ago, Mia had wandered off.

She now sat with her legs soaking in the heated swimming pool, her mind running off to a place I'd ask her about later. For now, I just wanted to look at her. Take in her beauty. Her calming presence.

Meeting McKenzie had rattled her and my thoughts ran rampant at the kind of conversation they'd had. I didn't want Zie to encroach on our time again. Digging up a painful past had no benefit for either of us.

I rose from the lounger and headed off toward her, rounding the pool.

I kicked off my shoes, removed my socks, and rolled up my

pants before taking a seat beside Mia. It felt good to dip my feet in the water. This welcome warmth took the edge off the cool air.

I nudged her arm playfully. "I've turned on the Jacuzzi."

Her gaze settled on Richard. "I think I'll go home."

A jolt of uncertainty hit me like a fucking train wreck.

"No," she said, reaching for my arm and giving it a squeeze. "The beach house."

Relief flooded in and another wave of guilt settled low in my gut for what I'd done. Yet there was Richard, sipping champagne and seemingly happy enough. I had a lifetime of making it up to him.

"Mia, you're staying here tonight."

"You and Richard need alone time. I'll never forgive myself if I ever cause any friction between you."

"No," I said, "you hold no responsibility for how everything turned out. None whatsoever."

"I feel as though I do."

I let out a long sigh, refusing to relent.

"I'll take you up on the Jacuzzi offer another night, though," she said. "Sounds heavenly."

"This is your home now."

"When I moved in with Richard, things went wrong," she whispered.

"That was different."

Her gaze swept over the house.

"We'll hang out in the den," I said.

"It's like you're separate from all this. I want to be with you. I need you. But this—" She swept her hand through the air. "It's a lot to take in."

"You'll get used to it."

"I'll stay tonight," she said. "Tomorrow we'll talk about it, okay?"

It wasn't okay, but this conversation was best confronted after a good night's sleep. We were still reeling after this morning's reunion.

And that party had put a damper on tonight.

"Mia, what did McKenzie say to you?"

Her attention shifted to the water but she wasn't really looking at it.

"Hey Cam!" Richard called over. "I'm going to borrow one of your spare bedrooms."

"Of course," I said. "Put Leo in the gold suite."

Richard laughed. "I've got him a car home." He threw us a wave. "Night, Mia."

"Goodnight, Richard," she called over affectionately.

He gave a nod of reassurance and led Leo inside.

"That was nice of you to invite Leo," she said.

"Being around you is making me soft."

"Hardly. Is Richard all right?"

"I think so."

"Please spend time with him soon."

"We'll always be close." I turned to face her. "We were talking about McKenzie?"

"She told me you're a good man."

"And?"

Mia's stare met mine. "McKenzie told me you're not the marrying kind."

"Ah."

"You left her at the altar?"

I reached over and tipped her chin up. "Mia, it was three weeks before the wedding. Which I know is no better. It was hard on us both."

"She was your one true love. The one you told me about at Chrysalis."

"You're my one true love."

"Why wouldn't you say her name before?"

Because her name brings back that vision of Zie in the Harrington Suite...

Ruined.

All of it.

Love, decimated.

"It's still painful," I muttered. "I hurt her. That hurts me."

"She's very pretty. Sophisticated."

"So are you."

"I'm a southern belle with a smart mouth," she said. "No Ivy League in sight. I imagine your friends wonder what you see in me."

"Don't Mia, and for the record everyone adores you."

"You're super smart, Cameron. What if you get bored with me?"

I held back on a frown and put her insecurities down to her age. Mia's confidence was still shaky, her innocence enduring. "I could say the same about you, Mia. I'm a stern master."

"I love that about you."

I gave a crooked smile. "And I love that you love that about me."

"McKenzie's so...perfect."

No, she was not.

"It's no mystery why we didn't work out," I said "We didn't share the same vision for our future."

Of course the correct answer was Zie wasn't perfect, but the fact was other than my distaste of her debutant lifestyle we'd been happy. It wasn't like I'd given up the luxurious life I'd been born into. I too enjoyed the finer things in life so couldn't really accuse Zie of living decadently. I'd always struggled with privilege. McKenzie had been caught in the wake of my search for self-discovery. My need for meaning. Purpose. My eventual desire for purity.

Zie's reservations about my philanthropic endeavors could have been resolved and she'd excelled within the S&M lifestyle, taking hedonism to an entirely new level. She was the kind of woman any man would have considered the ultimate prize. There was no appeal in a trophy wife though, not even one as gorgeous as Zie.

Mia shifted uncomfortably. "You proposed to her in Paris?"

"How long did you chat for?" I feigned amusement.

"A while. McKenzie told me you met at Chrysalis."

Yes, we had.

Months later, Zie and I had flown to Paris to spend time at Le Fernier's Maison de Plaisir, where she'd undergone extensive submissive training. That small scar on her upper back was evidence of her demand to be pushed further.

I recalled her begging us not to leave Le Maison after being immersed at the highest level. She, like so many submissives, had become infatuated with the sexual freedom it had brought her. She'd morphed into an erotic beauty and was hailed as an authority on all things amorous. Under my tutelage Zie had flourished, setting both Le Maison de Plaisir and the social scene ablaze with her extraordinary love of exhibitionism and her desire to experiment. I'd found her bi-sexuality endearing.

During those long, breathtaking days, it had been impossible to imagine life without her. Inevitably Zie and I had moved in together and our relationship had quickly evolved. Before leaving France, I'd asked her to marry me.

In time, she'd demanded more.

The walls of obligation had closed in and I'd felt like I was the one collared. We'd burned through too many intensive nights of wild sex and I'd glimpsed her need to top, her secret wish to dominate me.

Yeah, not gonna to happen.

I refused to relent to anyone's control.

Ever.

I'd refused her need to rule and inevitably pushed Zie away.

And ended *us.*

I'd rendered a soon-to-be bride devastated and a submissive without a master.

The very weekend our marriage was supposed to have taken place I'd flown off to Tibet. Alone. Remaining behind was too damn painful and I'd needed to get far away, put distance between me and the devastation I'd caused. Zie accused me of making her a social pariah and solidifying my reputation as a playboy.

We'd not seen each other until tonight.

All those memories came screeching back in all their glorious dysfunction, like the car wreck we'd once been. All that pain, all that disappointment, all that yearning for peace I'd failed to obtain when around her.

Upon my return from the East, I'd gone on the ultimate bender within the club scene with Richard and Shay at my side, and it was hard not to smile as I recalled us reigning supreme at Chrysalis. All three of us left a slew of wanton submissives in a wake of euphoria. Our preeminence brought us exhilaration and forged our reputations as Lords of Chrysalis.

After Zie, there'd been no one.

A self-imposed ban.

Subs need only apply. I'd train them, sure, and then give them back. The women were brilliant reflections of my special brand of skills.

Until *her.*

That stunning creature sitting beside me who'd bewitched me with her heady combination of innocence and sensuality. The one woman who always knew what I needed and responded flawlessly to any pleasure or punishment I bestowed.

Even now, obediently sitting silently beside me and allowing me to get lost in my own thoughts, her hand rubbing my back with affection.

I struggled to believe I deserved this kind of happiness.

Mia brushed her fingertips along her collar. "I know that this means you own me...but..."

Rising out of this melancholy, I realized where Mia was going with this. "Yes?"

"McKenzie told me I'm merely your property," she said. "Like one of your paintings."

I smirked. "I actually own several priceless pieces."

She still looked uncertain.

"Mia, have I not confessed my love for you? Risked so much for us to be together?"

"But what kind of love, Cameron?"

"What do you want me to say, Mia?"

She had every right to ask this. I'd seduced her away from her first love.

Mia broke my stare.

I didn't want Zie's poison anywhere near us.

"Let's not talk about her anymore." I refused to have tonight tainted.

"Do you see a future for us?"

Trying and failing to form the words she needed to hear, I shifted uncomfortably. My feelings were hard to define because I'd not felt this way about anyone. She was a perfect balance between feisty and submissive. This, *this* was sweet, sweet agony ravaging my every thought, and every breath felt like it belonged to Mia.

I reached over and unclipped her collar and removed it.

Her hand snapped up to her throat in a panic.

"Your trust in me proves your worthiness to wear *my* collar."

Mia grabbed it and pushed herself to her feet. She walked off toward the house.

Cursing Zie's interference, I pulled my legs out and rolled my pants back down.

Pushing to my feet, I headed after her.

Mia saw she had my attention and ran off into the house.

I took after her, adrenaline forging through my veins as I made quick headway into the house, down the hallway, flying around the corner, and bolting into the foyer.

This need to chase her alighted every cell in my body.

I ascended the staircase, taking two at a time, these intricately wired neurons firing my need to catch her.

Then fuck her.

Hard.

I grabbed hold of Mia's waist and swept her into my arms and she knew well enough not to struggle, hugging her collar into her chest. I carried her back down and along the hallway, toward that ordinary looking doorway and through it, down the winding staircase.

We descended into the climate controlled lowest level of the house.

I eased Mia down, grabbed her hand, and pulled her behind me, all the way along the sprawling chandelier lined corridor. She looked up at the dangling crystal droplets, seemingly mystified this place existed.

"Mia, next time I bring you down here you'll be crawling on your hands and knees," I chastised. "Understand?"

She sucked in a gasp of excitement. "Yes, master."

I punched in the ten digit code to get us in to what lay beyond—

The Vault.

CHAPTER 6

DELICATE RUBIES IN Mia's collar caught the light.

I'd rested it on a red velvet pillow atop the side table so she could see it from where I'd stood her at in the center, secured and bound. Stripped of her dress, she merely wore her bra and panties. Her arms were outstretched on either side of her, her wrists restrained in leather cuffs, but her ankles free.

This device was the Italian designer's take on a chrome Saint Andrew's Cross, only this one had moveable parts to ensure the sub could be placed in any stance a master desired. Strung up, legs splayed, bent over, or ass merely curved. The ultimate apparatus to ensure a sustained tension and the means to provide resistance free access from any angle.

Mia looked beautiful standing upright and held captive against the gold plated arms of the device. Her cheeks were flushed, her breaths came short and sharp, and her breasts rose and fell with each gasp. Those blonde locks cascaded over trembling shoulders. Her pensive expression fired my dark need to pleasure her in the midst of her confinement.

I stripped off my shirt and stood barefoot before her.

Watching. Waiting. Gaging.

Following her gaze as she looked around.

Chrome walls, foreign accruements that she'd have no idea about, that low hung blue droplet chandelier in the center throwing off a glittering light. That four poster bed I'd let her sleep on later.

Perhaps. Or maybe I'd keep her awake and not waste a second of having her in here.

Her frown proved she was wondering about that red door at the end and where it led.

"This room is sacred," I told her. "It belongs to us. And us alone. There will be no talk of the world outside while we are in here. Or anyone other than us. Do you understand?"

She gave a nod.

"You have a question?"

She lowered her gaze.

I neared her and rested a fingertip beneath her chin and raised her head to look at me. "You're asking for proof of my love?"

She gave off a mixture of nervousness and anticipation—swooning.

"Mia, while we are in here you are my property. In here, I own you. You will do what I tell you without hesitation. Am I making myself clear?"

"Yes, sir."

A thrill ran up my spine to see her entering subspace.

I pointed to her collar. "What does this mean?"

She hesitated.

"Mia." I reached around her waist and ran my fingertips up her spine. "The sub who wears my collar will be worshiped, cherished, spoiled, nurtured, protected, punished, and pleasured beyond all understanding."

She trembled against me.

"In here you are my property, yes, and you have every right to fear me. I am a stern master and will expect the very best from my sub." I pointed upward. "Up there, out in the world, you will wear my collar. It represents you are mine. I will share everything I have with you. I will listen to you, anticipate your needs, and give you everything you want to be happy and fulfilled."

Her eyelashes flickered. "Your girlfriend?"

I kissed her nose. "My lover. Everyone will know you are mine. Such a position carries status and power."

I could see in her eyes she wanted to know if we'd ever be more. We weren't there yet, and I wasn't sure we'd ever be. Mia's fear of abandonment proved she needed the kind of reassurance only a proposal could carry.

My passion was intense and it wasn't the first time a woman needed reassurance that this level of emotion would endure—a physical relationship that fulfilled a woman entirely.

I'd once been told that after the time spent with me was over it felt like the equivalent of drowning for the sub. The reality of finding a master with my exact talents was rare apparently, leaving women starved of that which they'd be exposed to. Refusing to hold back on the blinding pleasure I'd bestowed on them didn't exactly make it easy.

The present moment drew me back.

I reached up and unclipped Mia's wrists, releasing her. "What do you desire?"

Mia stepped away and scurried over toward her collar. She lifted it off the pillow and placed it around her neck. She returned to me and spun around for me to secure the catch.

"Master." She knelt before me.

I moved away from her toward the light switch and dimmed the vault, setting the scene before strolling over to the walled wireless system. Hans Zimmer oozed from the surround sound speakers. A hypnotic, moody piece that filled the room with vibration.

Making my way back to her, I rested a hand on the top of her head. "Stand."

I grabbed Mia's bra and ripped it off her and it made her jolt. I knelt and did the same with her panties, leaving her naked and running a hand over the curve of her buttocks.

From the corner trunk, I removed the long strands of fine, strong rope. Taking my time, dissolving into the ritual, I began the process of binding Mia, using intricate geometric patterns around her curves, having mastered the art of Shibari a long time ago. This ancient form of Japanese bondage was once reserved for beloved prisoners. The technique was so complex and time consuming it was reserved only for our most cherished.

I weaved the last rope around her breasts. "Well done, kitten," I said huskily.

Mia swooned, that telltale soft blush on her chest proving she was rope drunk.

I continued on, binding her wrists together and then reaching for the four golden link chains hanging from the ceiling.

Clipping them methodically, two to her upper back and two to the rope encircling her hips, I secured her. Reaching up for the central chain and giving it a tug, she tilted face downward and her toes left the ground. This beautiful creature was suspended with her thighs parted, her panting revealing her adrenaline had spiked in her veins.

I yanked the main gold chain to my left and Mia jolted upward. Continuing to pull, Mia went higher still, until she hung twenty feet in the air.

I admired my handiwork of a floating beauty suspended midair. Her pussy flinched with excitement.

I called up to her. "If you ever break one of my rules again, this is how I will punish you."

"Yes, master." Her chest rose and fell with tiny rapid breaths.

"This," I said firmly, "is what it means to trust."

"Yes, sir."

I folded my arms across my chest. "I look forward to our future, Mia, and all that it promises to be."

"Thank you, sir."

God she was beautiful. Like a fine marble sculpture carved from the purest stone. Her back was to the ceiling while her front faced the floor. Golden locks tumbled over her face. She swayed in a slow steady rotation.

Twenty minutes later, I lowered her.

Mia's sweet expression of affection for me was exactly what I'd yearned to see. She'd fully understood the meaning of this lesson.

Her skin responded to the feather I used to tease her. I moved on to the Wartenberg Pinwheel, with its rotating evenly-spaced sharp pins, running it along her flesh and causing her to writhe. I took my time to flog her. All the while, I ensured she remained in subspace and those tell-tale signs of her sustained arousal were maintained—her dilated pupils, her constant groaning, thighs shaking, and the most obvious, her pussy, soaked and spasming in its own sweet way of begging.

I tipped her chin up to look into her eyes. "My sweet, angel."

"Please fuck me, sir."

"Patience."

I grabbed her hips, pulled her back, and let her go so she

swung like a pendulum.

Mia giggled.

I grabbed the rope and stilled her. "You find this funny?"

"No, sir, I like it. It's like flying."

Standing behind her so she couldn't see my grin, my guard lessened. I paced around her, pausing briefly to build the tension again, anticipation, her waiting for the inevitable—

She glanced back at me, the action causing her to swing slightly.

"Turn around," I commanded.

Running my hands over her thighs, the arch of her spine, I dragged my fingertips around to her front and lowered to her sex. "This is where your spiritual energy rises from. The base of awareness of your sacredness." I eased apart her lips and tapped two fingers upon her clit.

She exhaled in a rush, eyelids flickering.

"This delicate organ is devoted merely to pleasure. It represents the sacred feminine. This—" I tapped her clit again – "reflects love. Compassion. Service."

That little nub responded, twitching with delight as my pacing increased, my pressure insistent. Mia's thighs trembled, her cheeks flushed, her mouth went slack.

With a fingertip, I encircled her clit. "This is your birthright, Mia." I leaned into her ear. "Enjoy this as God intended. Through this, you will lose your sense of self. Connect with the infinite."

Her brow furrowed in that thoughtful way of hers.

"Who does this belong to?"

"You, sir."

"Say it."

"My clit belongs to you, sir."

"That is correct. Who do you belong to?"

"You, sir."

"By the swimming pool, you hinted this was not enough." I flicked her clit.

"I'm not sure what I meant now," she said breathlessly.

"Have I not told you I love you?"

"Yes, sir."

"I know what you need."

Her eyes moistened and her lips trembled with emotion.

"Your body is a temple and I take great pleasure in worshiping you. I will leave no doubt in your mind how I feel about you. However, first I will punish you for questioning me." I pinched her clit.

She let out a moan of pleasure as I traced a fingertip along her sex.

I retrieved from the wall rack that cat-o-nine tails with its thin cords and thick handle. After tapping it in my left palm before her, I dragged the soft leather straps along the small of her back, her abdomen, and across her breasts and along her collar bone.

I brought it up to her mouth and she suckled on the tip of the handle, her tongue rimming it, teasing, hinting what she wanted to do to me.

If I let her.

I started with gentle whips to bring her naked skin awake, providing hypnotic stings to her flesh, pinking it, warming, stimulating nerve endings and setting her neurons alight with the perfectly timed sensations.

Mia was lulled into a trance, her body moving in sync with each strike. Her thighs parted. Her hips arched forward in yearning for the caress of those thin cords.

I left her wanting, needing, her breaths short and sharp.

I gripped the chain above her and gave it a yank. I wasn't touching her, but Mia responded as though I was.

Leaning in to her ear, I whispered, "I am changed. I hardly recognize myself. All that I was seems inconsequential now." I yanked the central chain to bring her closer. "Mia, you believe you're the one bound. You're not really. I'm the one captured. By everything you say and do. All that you are."

She held my gaze, her eyes glistening in the dark.

"You are everything that is beautiful in this world. You shine brighter than any sun and your soul sings more profoundly than any sonnet. Your eyes haunt my dreams, Mia. You are beholden of a dazzling beauty, an ethereal presence that could possess any heart you desired. I am seduced completely, beguiled by your soft skin, so sensitive, so responsive. Your exquisite breasts, your nipples pert in their yearning to be pinched and suckled." My gaze lowered to her sex. "This delicate flower that even now responds to its master obediently, wet as it readies for me, your clit erect and needful of your Dom's firm mastering."

Her eyelids grew heavy, her body trembled toward her closeness.

Still not touching her, I continued to taunt her arousal, "Beneath my fingers, I'll strum you slowly, my submissive. Just how you like it."

She was too entranced to speak.

"Pleasure can also serve as a punishment. You ran away from your master. A sin. Your punishment will be me encircling your clit extraordinarily slowly, prolonging your chastisement. Until you scream for me to forgive you."

Her body trembled. Her eyes searched mine as though trying to understand how, without any physical contact, I was sending her over.

"Perhaps, if I'm feeling merciful, I'll allow you to come, kitten. If you are good. Can you be good?"

Mouth gaping, her climax building, the tension from the rope around her sex carried her over.

"I look forward to your impending clit play, Ms. Lauren. You've proven yourself worthy to deserve hours of concentrated dedication to it. You've earned yourself a slow steady flicking. A firm encircling. My tongue fucking you at the same time. Would you like that?"

Her face blushed wildly, jaw gaping.

"That's right, surrender," I said. "Come for me, my sweet submissive. I demand it, now."

Through small gasps, she climaxed, her thighs shaking, her eyes squeezed shut, her body twitching and trembling, her movement causing her to swing. Her face flushed brighter, and her expression showed confusion that she wasn't even being touched, but merely the power of my words had sent her over. Her expression grew euphoric, caught up, enraptured, limbs shuddering under the strain.

Her bliss had been captured over the centuries by artists, musicians, and poets, their ability to immortalize this sacredness encapsulated in their timeless work.

Mia's moans echoed around us.

She was coming still...

This lifestyle was nothing without trust between a master and his chosen one. Domination was the purest craft. One perpetuated control throughout the scene, leading one's submissive through a sacred cycle of both pleasure and pain to roll one orgasm into the other in an unbroken loop of ecstasy.

And so it was.

Utilizing the mechanism I'd captured her in, positioning her to widen her thighs and expose her further, I knelt behind her and leaned in, holding onto the rope on her ankles and pulling her toward me.

This was how to truly worship a woman, suckle upon her sex and kiss her tenderly, slowly at first and then sliding into a rhythmic tongue strumming. Her trembling proved she came again. Her juices covered my face and her scent marked me.

Teasing her with denial, planting kiss after kiss on her inner thighs, moving from one to the other, I nipped as I went.

She screamed, too far gone.

Returning to her sex, I lapped there until I'd taken all I wanted, as though only this might in some way quench my thirst for her. My cock ached, my heart soared over finding her.

Blinded by lust, I gave myself over to this searing pleasure, my erection so hard, so insistence, I could refuse this allure no longer. Rising to my feet fast, freeing myself from my pants, I quickly found her entrance. I slid inside, filling her completely until I'd buried myself so fully the tip nudged her womb. This position allowed for the deepest penetration.

Gripping the chain on either side of her hips, I used this for leverage to pound into her, driving her on with a fierceness, bringing her back onto my cock with an uncompromising force.

Mia's throaty cries drifted as her body went rigid and she came again, her muscles clenching around my shaft. My thoughts scattered like glass.

I was too gone to remember to breathe.

CHAPTER 7

AFTER FIVE MILES of pounding the pavement, I was ready to get back to Mia.

I'd left her sleeping in my bed.

The memory of our play in the vault during the early hours caused my cock to harden. This insatiable need saw no end in sight. I shook my head in amusement. No other sub had captivated me like this, not even close.

I could still smell her on me.

Heading back, I assured myself my usual brutal running pace would start up again, and maybe I'd even have Mia joined me. Richard had left early this morning before I'd gotten up. I'd texted him to call me. We needed to hang out again soon.

I'd given my housekeeper Helen the day off, as well as my butler Lincoln, so we'd have the place to ourselves.

Strolling the hallway toward the kitchen, I felt the difference already. I'd always ignored that nagging sense of loneliness enhanced by all this space, but here, now, the contrast emphasized what I'd willingly endured: a self-imposed solitude.

I'd found *her.*

The one.

I knew it in the depth of my soul.

Even if the journey had been harrowing, there was no doubt Mia was worth every angst filled moment until I'd been able to call her mine.

Unable to wipe this ridiculous grin off my face, I set about making us breakfast, preparing toast, eggs—sunny side up—and sausages. And a pot of coffee.

I carried it up to my bedroom, *our bedroom.*

Mia blinked awake and pushed herself up the headboard. She was disheveled, her locks knotted in a mass of blonde and falling over her face. Her wayward look was outrageous proof of our time in the vault. She peered with one eye open through golden strands.

"I take full responsibility for getting you tipsy," I said. "And as the cause I'm also responsible for the cure." I rested the tray on the bed and offered her two pain pills. "For your hangover."

"I don't have a hangover." She popped the pills into her mouth and picked up the glass of orange juice and sipped. "I'm just achy from that Olympic sport you call sex."

She made me chuckle.

"You went for a run?"

"I did, and as a merciful master I didn't make you go with me."

"That would have been fun to watch," she said. 'Me trying to keep up with you." She looked down at the tray. "My suspicions have been clarified. I did die and go to heaven last night."

"I did warn you." I poured piping hot coffee into the two mugs. "When you're in the vault, there will be certain expectations to adhere to. My rules. When out of there, I'll have the privilege of spoiling you."

She took the coffee and wrapped her hands around it.

"Careful," I said, pulling off my shirt. "It's hot."

She arched a brow as her stare roamed over my body.

"How'd you sleep?"

"Good, you?"

"Great."

"All I can think about is going back into your vault. Never thought those words would ever come out my mouth."

She blinked at me and it made me smile.

I sat beside her and buttered a slice of toast and then handed it to her.

"Thank you."

"I'm going to spend some time with Henry this morning."

Mia paused mid-bite and then relented with a nod.

"I'd love for you to come with me. If you like?"

"I would love that," she said brightly. "Sure you don't want some brother time?"

"Henry's looking forward to seeing you."

"Are we going to Venice Beach?"

"Yes. I told Henry the place is his. He's been secluded for so long. Venice is a real contrast."

"Perhaps he could come and live here?"

"He knows that." I tucked a strand of hair behind her ear.

She shifted her gaze to the wall where Thomas Rafael's portrait hung—a lighthouse in the middle of an East Coast storm. I'd found comfort in it.

She looked back at me. "I need to talk to you about McKenzie."

"If we must."

"McKenzie was curious about how you knew Andrea. I didn't tell her we gate-crashed. She wanted to know what you've been up to. I really did try to avoid her questions." Mia traced the edges of her collar. "She saw us arrive so she assumed I was your sub."

"Why hide in that closet?"

"Needed time to think."

"About?"

"Stuff."

"What did she say?"

"Apparently I'm not your usual type."

"My tastes have evolved. She wouldn't know that."

Mia took a bite of toast and chewed thoughtfully.

"Go on," I said.

"McKenzie told me I haven't begun to see your dark side, Cameron." Mia's eyes lowered. "She told me you're the most hedonistic man she's ever met."

"I own Chrysalis. That tells you everything."

"She told me…"

"Yes?"

"I'm your living fantasy."

"Well she got something right."

Mia's hand nervously massaged the comforter. "Do you have a cage?"

"Yes."

"Here?"

"Yes."

"Behind that red door? Are you going to lock me up in it?"

"The problem with Zie is her jealousy."

"You are, aren't you?" Her breath stilted. "You're going to lock me away and…"

"Cage work is part of our world, Mia."

She pushed the tray away.

"As my submissive, you must trust me to provide what is right for you. To know exactly what you need and provide it."

"I don't need that, Cameron."

I raised my glare to hers. "Clearly you do."

CHAPTER 8

THERE CAME A sinister joy in seeing Mia vulnerable, silenced.

She grabbed her pillow and pounded my head with it. "You're fucked up," she screeched playfully. "It's not right."

"What is it with you and pillows?" I reached for one myself and tapped her head with it. "And mind your language."

"I'm freaking out."

"And how beautiful you look."

"You're incorrigible."

"Careful."

She looked at me coyly.

"Better." I pulled her toward me, pressing my lips against hers and kissing her deeply, tasting coffee and juice as I swirled my tongue around hers, tasting Mia. I cupped her face in my hands. "Still trust me?"

"Always."

I hated Zie for interfering and hate was a rare emotion for me. My next call would be to warn her to stay away from Mia. To stay away from us both.

"So you enjoyed what happened in the vault?" I said.

"Yes," she burst out with excitement and nuzzled into me, her arms wrapped around my neck.

"Every piece in there is created for your enjoyment, Mia."

"I'm excited." She took my hands in hers. "Only..."

"What?"

"I'm not sure about exhibitionism?"

Mia had every right to ask that. I'd taken her on a brief tour of Chrysalis and showed her the way of the house. At a hedonistic party there, Mia witnessed two of our members in the throes of a public display of passion. Shay had accompanied us that evening and he too had joined the sexual fray and heated up the scene in spectacular fashion. At the time, Mia had accepted what she'd seen, though I'd had my hand down her panties to enhance her thrill and bring her into the sensual display.

What had followed that night was the most mind-blowing vanilla sex I'd ever had, proving Mia was an exceptional conquest. The rarest find. The way she submitted was the purest elixir, and when she pushed back in that feisty way all my cock knew was her.

She looked up at me, still waiting for my answer. "Cameron?"

"You're young now," I reassured her. "Perhaps later you'll crave variety? Want to experiment?"

She gave a wary nod.

"To be honest, Mia, this is new territory for me too. I'm not sure I want anyone looking at you."

"Have I tamed the great Cameron Cole?"

She earned herself a spanking.

It was a good thing the house was empty other than us. Her screams mixed with laughter would have brought the staff running. With her lying across my lap, her nightdress hitched waist high, my hand came down hard on her butt. She writhed and squirmed through her punishment.

"Obey," I demanded.

She stilled and settled into subspace.

Her reward was my lowered hand delivering softened strikes upon her pussy. The spanks sent her the rest of the way and she shuddered as she came.

"Thank you, master," she managed breathlessly.

"You are so very welcome." I delivered one final hard spank to her butt. "Don't joke about taming me, Mia. Understand?"

She gave a cautious nod.

I pounced on her and we tussled upon the bed sheets.

And it made me laugh.

We settled eventually, with Mia resting her head on my chest and me enjoying the quiet. Mia had this way of losing herself in her own thoughts with no need to fill the silence.

"Mia," I said softly. "I understand this is a delicate issue. I feel we should talk about it."

She raised her head to look at me.

"Your father," I said.

She knitted her brow together. "What about him?"

"Should you ever want me to arrange a reunion—"

"No. And please don't tell me the only way I'll ever become a truly self-actualized person if I resolve that part of my life."

"Perhaps we should explore your feelings?"

"It hurts."

"I wish I could take it away."

"I question why he left and didn't come back. It's hard to shake it. I go round and around trying to work out why…"

"Absolutely nothing. Taking the blame is usual for victims."

"You've helped me see it wasn't my fault, Cameron," she said. "I'm not sure I want him in my life. I choose to do what's healthy for me. That's my prerogative."

"He lost the privilege of knowing you. Any relationship would be on your terms."

It was good to see Mia opening up and we talked a little more, exploring her feelings and working towards soothing her heartache. We were some way off her healing, but it was a start.

With an unfamiliar serenity, sleep pulled me down again.

I stirred and raised my head to peer down to watch Mia sleep, trying to wrap my mind around the fact this exquisite young woman was really mine. Mia woke soon after and we wallowed in bed, stirring to greet what would start out as a leisurely morning. We showered together and it was a challenge to keep my hands off her.

Eventually we pried ourselves from the house.

I drove us to Venice in the Bentley convertible. We both went for casual, with me in jeans and a shirt and Mia in jeans too and a sweater she'd pulled from one of the suitcases that Richard had dropped off at my place earlier.

The remnants of Mia's life were stored away in boxes and several suitcases. They'd been left in the foyer for her to unpack later.

She'd stared at them warily on the way out and I'd reassured her we'd find a place for all her things. I wanted her settle in as soon as possible. Having Mia feel at home was my priority. I loved sharing all I had with her.

"Not sure my stuff goes with your stuff," she said.

"Well there's always Goodwill."

"How about we get rid of your stuff and keep my stuff."

"And have my interior designer on my case? I don't think so."

"Fire her."

"She's a he. How about this as a viable option? I pull the car over and spank you again?"

She twisted in her seat. "Will you always be this bossy?"

"Yes."

"How many cars do you own?"

I steered us onto Elevado Avenue. "I've lost count."

"That's silly."

She'd yet to see my subterranean collection of vehicles beneath the house.

"Not as silly as being gifted a BMW and giving it back."

She shifted to look at me. "Those were unusual circumstances."

"In what way?" But I knew.

"It's just that I'm without a car now."

"Deal's off I'm afraid. Now all you're getting is a 1999 beat up old Mini to replace your last one."

"That was a 2006."

"I should have paid more attention. Oh well." I beamed at her.

"Maybe I can borrow one of yours?"

"As if."

"Then you'll have to come with me to a car dealer."

"Choose a color."

"Really?" She squealed with delight and tugged on my shirtsleeve.

It made me laugh.

"We can't buy a brand new one though," she said. "A car loses its value as soon as you drive it off the lot. Like thousands." She glanced over at me. "You probably know that."

"I'm sure we can work something out."

She giggled and slid down the seat.

With a push of a button on the front screen, I said, "Call HQ."

Suri responded: *"Calling HQ"*.

"The house," came Dominic's gruff reply.

"Dom, good morning. You're on speaker. Mia's in the car."

"Good morning, Dr. Cole," said Dominic. "Good morning, Mia. I trust you had a wonderful New Year?"

"We did, thank you," I said. "How was yours?"

"Playful. Our bash at Chrysalis went without a hitch. You were missed, sir."

"Good to hear. Look, Dominic, I won't keep you long. I want you to enjoy your day, but I have an issue."

"Consider it dealt with."

I smirked at his confidence. As a loyal friend and attorney and the man who stood in for me at Chrysalis when I couldn't be there, he'd proven invaluable. "One word. Or should I say name."

"Go on."

I glanced over at Mia. "Carter."

"As in McKenzie Carter?" he said.

"Afraid so."

Mia's gaze rose to meet mine.

"I see," said Dominic.

"No further contact," I said. "That's my stipulation."

"We'll slam her with a restraining order."

"Let's proceed delicately."

"Delicately it is," he said. "Plans for today, Cam?"

"We're visiting Henry in Venice. You?"

"I have ponies to feed." He chuckled. "All in a day's work."

"Have fun."

"Well I'm here at your den of iniquity, so it's a surety."

I laughed and pressed the screen to hang up. "Mia, you didn't hear that last part."

She pressed her hand against her chest, her accent pure southern bell. "Why sir, I am shocked to my core. You're the devil himself."

"Guess what?" I reached for her hand and kissed it.

"What?"

"We're going to sleep together tonight," I whispered it.

Mia melted into her seat.

CHAPTER 9

MY HAND FOUND its way back to her.

It rested on her inner thigh then slid up her dress. Her silky skin was perfectly smooth beneath my touch.

Mia blinked at me. "Cameron, thank you for letting me visit Henry with you."

"Pleasure's all mine."

She was a breath of fresh air and a wonderful distraction from all the usual testosterone fueled business dealings I'd been engrossed in lately.

I'd spent the last few days taking a slew of conference calls with my father, owner and CEO of Cole tea and Tempest Coffees. We'd strategized together on the best way forward with the impending advertising campaign.

The shareholders had been getting antsy and the board of directors had all but placed the thumbscrews on my father, demanding he cut costs and improve profits.

My dad had always insisted the company take care of its employees and honor its charitable responsibilities, which had been a real influence on me. Charlie's Soup Kitchen in Santa Monica was testament to that. The small restaurant that served the homeless had been my first philanthropic endeavor. I'd started it in my twenties, so it held a special place in my heart.

Mia had expressed a desire to take more shifts there to help out, and though I didn't need any validation on why she was perfect for me, her desire to help others was it.

I'd built my life on that philosophy. My psychiatric practice in Los Angeles was thriving, though lately I'd been juggling too much. Mia was proving the best remedy. Her playfulness, her intuition to know what I needed and when, had turned my life upside down. All for the better.

Her interference in my older brother Henry's wellbeing when she visited him in Big Bear, and somehow tempted him out of seclusion, verged on a therapeutic miracle.

She really was my perfect little angel.

"I can't wait to see him," she said.

I marveled at her ability to pick up on my thoughts.

We drove the rest of the way with my hand refusing to let go of hers, and Mia relaxed and seemed soothed by my touch.

I parked the Bentley in the garage next to the house. We headed around to the front door.

I knocked, despite having a key, wanting Henry to know I respected his privacy. I'd given him this place and wanted him to know he was safe here.

The door flew open and a smiling Henry appeared. "You're late."

Mia knelt to greet Dex, who leapt onto her lap and greeted her with licks and brushes of his head, his tail wagging. Henry had always had a thing for Labradors.

A check of my watch confirmed we were in fact late. I'd told Henry we'd be here by 11AM. It was 11:05.

With an arch of a brow, I gave him a look of *seriously?*

Dex left Mia's lap and sprang over to me.

"Hello, boy." I scratched his chin and ran my fingers over his thick black coat.

Mia flew into Henry's arms to give him the biggest hug. "There was traffic," she explained, gazing up at him.

"You're forgiven."

We followed him into the living area and I scanned the place, needing to see evidence my older brother was okay. The room was tidy, perhaps a little too tidy, with his shoes lined up in the corner in a hint of compulsive disorder. But Henry had trained as a SEAL at WestPoint, and if there was one thing I knew about military training was order was the foundation of an officer's life.

I caught the family photos he'd placed on the fridge. A good sign. The blinds were open, removing my fear he might have slipped into a depression, and the ironed shirt and jeans he wore, along with those highly polished shoes, proved he'd been looking forward to our arrival.

Henry folded his arms.

He'd caught me.

"What's wrong?" asked Mia.

"My brother has a Sherlock fetish," said Henry.

I waved it off and made my way over to the kitchen. "Coffee?"

"Yes please," said Mia, heading over to the fridge for the milk.

Within a few minutes, I'd handed over piping hot mugs filled to the brim with Tempest coffee to Mia and Henry, and we carried our drinks into the small garden. We made ourselves comfortable on the patio seating. I was reminded again why I loved this place. This beachside town was a reflection of the best life had to offer.

When I spotted that soft plaid blanket on the back of a lounger, I lifted it and carried it over to Mia, laying it over her legs to keep her warm. The morning chill lingered. She snuggled beneath it.

Venice was already thriving with eclectic energy. Beyond the pathway that ran along the back of the property was the view of a golden sandy beach, and beyond that ocean. Off to our right a basketball game was underway. A small crowd had gathered to watch. Surfers were taking advantage of the swell.

"How are you finding the noise?" I asked Henry.

"Doesn't bother me."

At night, tourists strolled along the boardwalk. I'd been surprised when Henry had told me he wanted to stay here and not at my Beverly Hills home, but he'd lived alone for so long and told me he didn't like the idea of bumping into my staff.

"Heard you had fun with Shay on his new boat?" I said.

"Yeah, he and Arianna invited me." He smirked. "She tried to set me up with her girlfriend but she was way too young."

"You always did go for older women," I said, smiling.

He tilted his head and grinned at Mia.

Yes, thank you for that, Henry. Since our days at boarding

school, he'd known about my penchant for women wearing tartan skirts and FMB's who liked nothing more than being mastered.

Funnily enough, the first time I'd been intimate with Mia she'd been wearing that very outfit. I'd made her come in front of Richard and we'd both been left bewitched by the girl with no idea of the power she held.

Glancing over at Mia, I wondered if my obsession would ever end. My body stiffened telling me a definitive *no*.

"I want to introduce Henry to Scarlet," said Mia.

My brows shot up with the thought of Scarlet and Henry in the same room. Henry wouldn't submit to any woman, even a sophisticated dominatrix like Scarlet Winters. Though she would be intrigued by the challenge.

"Any chance she might be a switch?" Henry's lip curled.

"She is," said Mia, looking over to me for confirmation.

A term Henry learned during his visit to see me at Harvard. I'd shamelessly displayed my collection of books on BDSM.

With me, all the domina's at both Enthrall and Chrysalis relented their power, but that was unusual for the scene. That kind of trust and respect had been earned. I ruled over Chrysalis with a firm hand but honored their power. They really were like a second family to me.

"I can talk with Scarlet?" I went along with Mia's meddling with a smirk. "If you like?"

"Sure," said Henry.

The scent of ocean and fresh coffee filled the air.

"We need to talk," he said.

"About?"

Henry arched a brow. "*It.*"

"Come on, big brother." My tone was laden with affection. "Let's surf."

CHAPTER 10

FOR CHILDREN BORN into an empire, their '*it*' is the threat of inheriting the seat of power looming over their heads since childhood.

No matter their own dreams, loves, or wants, their destiny is set. Dad had allowed Henry his brief foray in the military and my 'dabbling in medicine,' but there'd been an understanding we'd eventually leave behind our reckless bachelor ways and take up the honor of ruling the billion dollar domain known throughout the world as Cole Tea and Tempest Coffee. Our family franchise ranked at the top of the fortune 500.

The price was my dad's unwavering dedication to maintain the company's position at any cost and his lack of attention while we were finding our way in the world. With both Henry and I being sent off to boarding school at age five, Dad had already influenced us in ways both powerful yet vague.

We'd made our way through the wreckage of our lives to flourish, despite it all. Henry had been there for me every time I'd needed him. No matter what.

This wasn't about us not appreciating our privileged position. It was about us having to lay aside our life's calling.

Right on cue, Henry's surfboard crashed into mine.

God, I loved my brother.

It was wonderful seeing him this happy. There was nothing like cold water to shake me back to reality. My feet landed on the seabed and I grabbed the edge of my board to stop it floating away.

"Where were you just now?" he called over.

I gave a look of apology.

Henry slapped my back and leaped onto his board, paddling out.

Mia was still in the beach house curled up on the sofa. I'd put on an old favorite 1940 black and white movie, *The Philadelphia Story*. She was happy enough cuddling with Dex and relaxing. She knew we needed alone time. She'd waved us off with that glint in her eye. The brothers were spending time together.

A large wave headed our way and Henry took advantage of it, leaping onto his board, crouching low and surfing all the way in. He'd picked this up fast and it reminded me how alike we were. We'd both been groomed from an early age in numerous sports, me preferring polo, swimming, and tennis, and Henry showing a talent for football. He'd even been drafted into the navy league.

Another wave rolled toward us and with the nose of my board facing the beach I was ready. I leaped on and paddled, thrilled with being lifted by the water. I rose up with my weight above the center. The pull of the wave signaled to stand as I placed my left foot forward for balance.

A burst of adrenaline. My heartbeat raced and my lungs filled with fresh air. All thoughts were pushed aside as I zoned out—

Into the rush.

This, this was freedom, a sense of connection...

The purest nirvana.

After an hour, the ocean waves settled and Henry and I straddled our boards and sat opposite one another. The land was within easy reach. Rocked by the water, we sat like that for a while. Quiet. Thoughtful. Enjoying being close to each other again.

"He's not getting any younger," said Henry.

"He has our full support."

"Cam," he said, "Dad's under tremendous pressure. I talked with him on the phone last night. The business world is changing."

"I get that. Did you run by him the idea of Willow coming onboard?"

Henry gave that knowing look.

I answered my own question, "He's concerned she won't survive the boardroom."

"I'm ready to don a suit and get my hair cut."

"Go work for Dad?" Stunned, I looked over at him. "Well that's good." The weight of responsibility lifted off me.

"Still, I'm not the man I was before Afghanistan," he said. "We both know that."

"Not the man?"

He rolled his eyes.

"Sorry."

"That's okay, Doc. Just not with me."

"Of course."

"I've been groomed for the corporate world," he said. "My military experience was a conduit to that."

But life had other plans—the cruelest.

"After all I've been through," he said. "This will be a cinch."

I cringed inwardly as the memory came flooding back of seeing the state Henry was in after his SEAL taskforce extraction. And what those terrorists had done to him. Closing my eyes, I tried to squeeze out those images.

Though for Henry, who'd lived the nightmare, those memories would have seeped into his very marrow. I'd hardly recognized him as the doctors worked on him in that medical tent. Their initial first aid was administered in deathly quiet so as not to stress him further, considering he'd been in solitary confinement for months and the only respite from silence was being dragged out by his captors to be tortured.

That suffocating desert heat.

I'd stood back and waited for the military surgeons to be ready for me. A nod from them signaled it was my turn to be with my brother beneath that windblown camouflaged canopy. Not to comfort him. Not to soothe, but to cajole out of him the intel he'd gathered before his capture. The kind that saved lives.

'*Whatever it takes*,' had been General Daniel Newton's order.

As though the man using every last psychological trick he could muster to recover deeply embedded information wasn't Henry's brother.

Mission accomplished.

A man ruined. No, not just any man. My brother.

We'd flown out of there in a SEAL Stealth helicopter and I'd stared out the window and down at the country that had left two brothers forever wrecked.

Henry had given up the intel, but his sanity had gone with it.

Up until yesterday, I'd blamed myself for ruining his life, decimating his psyche. Every day I'd lived with the guilt of betraying his trust.

Yet here, now, we were together as brothers again, and the profoundness of being reunited and his unwavering forgiveness meant everything.

He stared at the beach, calmly watching the meandering tourists. It was hard to tell he'd ever endured all that. He had a serenity, a gratitude, that came with surviving a trauma. Even now he smiled at me in a way that expressed he loved me no less.

Those dark days would always stay with me.

"I'm so sorry," I said.

"Haven't we had this conversation?"

"You're not just telling me what I need to hear, Henry?"

"I don't remember much about it," he said. "I remember this though. You flew to Afghanistan and put your own life at risk."

"That was nothing."

"It was everything. I chose my career. What good was that intel stuck in my head?" He waved his hand through the air. "I'd have done the same to you, Cam. Ever considered that?"

I shrugged and gave him a consolatory glance.

He turned to look at me. "Dad believes your guilt might turn out rather handy."

"Ever the optimist."

"Apparently the boardroom is the equivalent of going to war." His face was marred with confusion.

"Are you sure you want this?'

"Yes."

"I just want you to be happy."

"At least Dad will be off your case now."

I reached over and tapped his shoulder. "We both needed this."

"Mia's a sweet girl, Cam. I like her. I really do."

I shook my head. "She went rogue when she visited you."

"Sounds like someone I know."

"What did you two talk about?"

"That'll be our little secret."

"Well, whatever it was I'm glad." I narrowed my gaze. "I'm thrilled you're going to stay."

He shrugged. "Do you think Mia's the one?"

I took in the horizon, with its endless vision of possibilities. "Yes, I do."

"Your cold bachelor heart melting?"

"I'm just as surprised."

"Mom and Dad are flying in on Friday," he said. "They can't quite believe I'm out of Big Bear."

I gave his back a pat and hugged him.

"I've booked a table at The Ivy," he said.

"Well they've already met Mia, so it shouldn't be too awkward."

"They'll ask about your engagement."

The announcement that had meant to save my ass was now threatening it. The last thing I needed was my mother on my case wanting to start planning a big wedding.

Henry nodded toward the beach and I saw Mia heading toward us. She was carrying two beach towels.

"If you ever consider joining me," he said. "I'm sure we can find you an intern position."

I laughed. "To be honest, it's frightening to think what business would bring out in me."

"Oh I know."

I arched a brow.

"That part of you that's willing to burn the empire down." He slapped my back. "Maybe it is best you stay away, Cam."

"You're more than capable of dragging the company into the twenty-first century."

"You'd probably blow the whole thing up."

We both laughed at that.

Pulling our boards with us, we waded out of the water. Once on dry land, I threw my board down, ran over to Mia, and scooped her up into my arms, kissing her.

Her sundress was soaked with seawater, but she didn't care.

"Did you have fun?" She beamed at us.

"Cam's going to teach you to surf next, Mia," said Henry.

"Now that should be interesting," she said.

"Who's hungry?" I picked up my board.

The three of us headed off across the sand toward Bradley's Bistro. The restaurant sat between a rustic tattoo parlor and an old book store. We rested our boards outside the front against the wall and headed on in. There were traces of sand trodden in and it felt perfect for a low key get together. The rickety tables and well-worn furnishing left formality behind. It was easy to spot the servers who were wannabe actors. They held a certain glazed stare as they dreamed their day away. The laidback surfer staff were easy to spot. They were here just to support their freewheeling lifestyle, their frequent gazes toward the ocean revealing their yearning.

The scent of pot wafted over our table.

Henry arched a brow when he caught it. "Good choice." He widened his eyes in amusement.

"I thought so," I said, amused, pulling back a chair for Mia.

We settled at a corner table and each chose taco's off the menu. We sipped on lime beer. The brief moments of quiet proved how comfortable we all were with each other. The relaxed mood was easy to settle into.

Our conversation went from how great the surf was down here, to Henry sharing stories of his days in the SEALS. Mia was wowed as Henry recalled his experiences in the Middle East. Having already shared with her some of his darkest history when she visited him in Big Bear, Henry seemed comfortable to open up further.

Now and again Mia asked him a question that provided even more insight into what he'd been through and how his life had change since leaving the military. Henry told us he'd been dating a young lieutenant before his deployment to Afghanistan.

"Secret missions have a way of compromising relationships," he said flatly.

"Like James Bond." Mia tried to cheer him up.

"I wish. Talking of Bond, any plans for your future, Miss Money Penny?"

Mia giggled and took another bite out of her taco.

"You can't work for my brother indefinitely."

I took a swig of beer and looked over at her.

"I'm considering attending the psychology program at UCLA," she said.

I beamed full of pride. "You have a place at UCLA waiting for you."

"I don't want you pulling strings, Cameron," she said.

I looked over at Henry. "Tell her strings are good. Strings make the world go round."

"Well if you change your mind," he said, "I know a great company hiring young executives. The salary's great. The benefits are generous and the camaraderie amongst the staff rocks. You can join the baseball team."

"She doesn't want to work for dad," I said.

"She'd be working for me." He lowered his gaze at her. "You'd get to travel, Mia."

"Are you headhunting my girlfriend?"

"And now that your girlfriend is an executive with the company, you might want to come on over to the dark side yourself."

"I haven't accepted the offer yet," Mia muttered and looked over at me.

"You gave a nod." Henry raised his beer bottle in congratulations.

"I was taking a bite of food."

"Looked like a signed and sealed acceptance of a job offer to me," he said.

Mia and I laughed.

Mia beamed at him. "Shouldn't I be formally interviewed?"

"You just were."

"She's going to UCLA, Henry," I said.

"Maybe I will accept," she said. "Will I get a car?"

"Look at you," said Henry. "You're not in the job five minutes and you're demanding executive upgrades."

"If you are serious," she said, "and I'm not so sure you are, but if you are, thank you for considering me."

"Well there you have it, Mia," I said. "Your future just opened up."

Henry gave a nod. "And now you, sir. Time to close that den of iniquity before dad finds out about your extracurricular activities."

I flipped a coaster at him and he failed to dodge it.

"Let's go back to the house," I said. "I have just the thing to prepare you for your future, young one." I gestured to our waiter for the check.

"Go on then. Let's have it," Henry said.

"I may have an old monopoly board in my cupboard."

"I knew it," said Mia, "I knew you'd have a thing for that game."

I signed the check and then nudged the leather wallet to the side.

Henry looked over at Mia. "Great drinking game."

"Never played it."

Henry feigned horror and then pointed at me. "This one's obsessed with it."

"When I was twelve," I said. "It's actually not mine. It's Tara's."

Henry glanced over at Mia cautiously.

"It's okay," she said. "Tara's gay. She's dating my best friend, Bailey. Tara and Cameron surf together sometimes."

"Haven't for a while," I said. "My old surfing buddy's been too busy with her studies."

"She's studying to be a nurse," Mia told him. "Bailey's already graduated. She works at Cedars."

"Cameron always insisted he was the top hat." Henry pushed himself to his feet. "That's all you have to know about this one right here. One classy act."

"When I was a kid," I said. "Didn't you always go for the candlestick?"

"Different game." Henry rolled his eyes. "Yeah, try to pretend you weren't Mr. Mogul obsessed back in the day."

Mia rose to her feet. "So I take it Cameron always ended up winning?"

"Always." Henry looked over at me. "Too smart for his own good."

I pressed my hand to my chest. "I'll play, but only if I'm the top hat."

"That piece mysteriously disappeared last night," said Henry mischievously.

"Well, we need to sharpen your business strategizing ability," I said. "So monopoly it is."

We'd not been this playful in years. So much time had gone

by where we'd let life get in the way. I vowed that would not happen again to us.

We made our way out onto the pathway.

Mia knelt to play with a Maltese puppy and she grinned up at the pet's owners. The middle aged couple were more than happy to have their dog admired.

"Someone's got it bad," said Henry, his lips curling wryly.

"What?" I said, pretending I'd not stared down at Mia like a lovesick teenager.

Mia's windswept hair reminded me of that freshly fucked look she had after one of our mind-blowing sessions. Her face had been kissed by the sun, and her blue eyes shone with happiness. She exuded sweetness.

She glanced our way. "Can we get one?"

"Sure," I said. "How about a coyote?"

She giggled and went back to petting.

It was hard to believe she'd ever had a bad day in her life. Yet here was a woman whose childhood could have rendered her full of hate for the world. Instead, she emanated love, and her endearing kindness captured my heart. It was impossible to understand how anyone could hurt her.

"First comes the dog," said Henry. "Then the baby."

I went to protest, but for the first time in my life I wasn't horrified by the thought. As though some part of me knew with Mia it would be fun, and she'd make an incredible mother.

That shimmer of peace felt closer than it ever had. I knew I had what was needed to make her happy. Equaled by the knowledge I had what it took to protect her.

That collar was no longer enough.

Henry wrapped his arm around me. "Had you not gotten that intel out of me," he said. "All that suffering, all that pain, all that agony I went through would have been for nothing. Ever considered that?"

Emotion strained my voice. "Henry."

CHAPTER 11

MIA SPUN AROUND for me, giggling and showing off the short black evening dress.

Sitting here in Badgley Mischka's store waiting room, I gave an appreciative nod, admiring the way she playfully posed.

God, she was beautiful.

There came a sense of pride I'd be with her tonight.

Scarlet's birthday party was this evening at The Strand, and I'd brought Mia to Rodeo Drive to buy her a new dress. Despite her owning quite a few, all of them had been purchased for her by Richard. I didn't feel comfortable with him seeing her wearing any of them and I didn't need any reminders she'd once been his.

She fell onto my lap. "I love this one."

I hugged her softness into me and nuzzled into her neck. Soft blonde curls caressed my face and I breathed her in. Her eyes shone with happiness.

And that made me deliriously happy. "Mia, you look beautiful." I glanced over at the shop assistant. "We'll take it."

Mia reached for the price tag and frowned. "Maybe we should go to the mall?"

"Looks like someone's going to have to work overtime," I said, amused.

"What will be my duties?"

"Whatever they are, you will be naked. There's no way around it."

She kissed me. "It's beautiful. Thank you so much."

"It's nothing." I reached into my pocket for my cell and went to silence it and saw Shay's name. "I should get this. Go find your shoes."

Mia headed on over to the elegant display—a collection of pumps, and heels, and wedges.

"Cole." I pushed to my feet and moved over to the front window.

"Hey boss," said Shay warmly.

"How are things?"

"Good. You?"

"Great. How's the boat?"

"Handles like a dream."

"Heard you took Henry out on it?"

"He seemed to have fun."

"A nice reunion, I hear?"

"Yeah, we bored the hell out of Arianna talking about old times. She kept trying to tempt us to swim." He chuckled. "We've lost our edge, Cam. Neither of us wanted to face the cold."

"You're getting old, buddy."

"Tell me about it."

"That'll be all the champagne and high rolling you do."

"You're a bad influence."

A car alarm went off and I pulled the phone away from my ear. "Where are you?"

"China Town. Arianna likes this little joint down here. Food's not bad, but to be honest her favorite dish looks like it's gonna bite back."

"Hang in there."

"Everything's set for tonight." His tone changed. "I booked a private room. VIP lounge."

"Sounds perfect."

"You pay me for perfection."

"And I thank you for always delivering it." I turned to see Mia staring out the window.

I froze.

Terror was etched on her expression.

"I'll call you back." I hung up and followed her gaze.

Tourists ambled by.

A man wearing sunglasses seemed to be peering through the shop window. His head tipped, his face hidden beneath a Carolina Panther's cap. He turned and walked toward a black Kia and climbed in. I didn't have time to catch the plate.

Mia's gaze shifted to mine. "It doesn't fit right." She hurried into the changing room.

My stare shot back to the street.

I followed her, finding Mia with the dress off and pulling on her jeans and shirt. Her eyes didn't meet mine.

I leaned against the wall with my arms folded, going for relaxed as a way to get her to calm and open up, all the while scrutinizing her.

She forced a smile and I forced one back.

"It's too expensive." She nodded to herself. "Doesn't fit right."

"It looked lovely on you."

The shop assistant appeared and I gestured for her to give us a minute.

"Another client needs the changing room," said the girl.

"One minute," I said.

"She's one of our regulars."

"She'll live." I turned to Mia. "Did you see someone you recognized?"

Mia stared at the wall. "It's just all too much, Cameron. You buying all this stuff for me." She lowered her voice. "It makes me feel dependent on you. I'm not used to it."

Well that was inaccurate for a start. Richard had spoiled her.

"Sir, perhaps if you don't mind stepping out," said the shop girl again.

"Perhaps I might buy the store," I said dryly. "And fire you."

She hurried out and I stepped forward to help Mia tug down her t-shirt. "Tell me why your demeanor changed so rapidly."

"I just became overwhelmed."

Her pupils dilated. Fine hairs prickled on her forearms. The inability to swallow. A soft blush on her neck. I'd caught every sign of a fight or flight response.

I leaned over and kissed her forehead. "We don't need to buy the dress."

She seemed to take comfort in that and sat to slide into her boots.

"Meet me outside," I said warmly.

I stopped on the way out to say to the shop assistant, "I was an ass. I apologize." I gave a courteous smile to her and the woman next to her, the client who was in a hurry to try on some chiffon number she held on a hanger.

"You can stay in there if you like," said the thirty-something woman, her eyebrows raised flirtatiously. The tip of her tongue rested on her upper lip suggestively.

With a polite wave, I left the store and took out my phone.

Shay's voice came on the other end. "If you're calling to tell me not to eat the entrails," he said dryly, "too late."

I caressed my forehead, half amused and half on a mission. "Sounds delicious, Shay. Listen, I need you to obtain security footage."

"Sure."

"Rodeo Drive. More specifically the camera's trained on Badgley Mischka."

"What or who am I looking for?"

"Can you get the name of the owner of a black Kia that was parked outside?" I glanced at my watch. "Male. White. Thirtyish, maybe. Soon as you can."

"I'll run his face through the recognition software we don't own."

"Thank you, Shay."

"What happened?"

"Nothing yet."

"Cole, let me deploy my security. I can have a team on you in fifteen."

I turned to look back inside. Mia was talking to the shop girl. She seemed a little calmer.

"Let's compromise," I said. "Have your men track Mia."

"I can do that."

"I trust her. Just don't trust the wolves, Shay."

"No one's getting near her."

"Your best men. I don't care what it takes."

Mia headed out onto the pavement. She looked a little sheepish. What the hell was guilt doing etched on her face?

"Hey there." I covered my hand over the phone. "Change of

heart on the dress?"

With a shake of her head, she told me she was going to be stubborn. It meant she'd be wearing something Richard had bought her tonight.

Fuck.

I opened the passenger door and she avoided my gaze as she climbed in.

Pulling the phone back to my ear, I said, "Shay, no room for error." I killed the call and joined her in the car.

The engine idled as I sat for a moment, pretending to scroll through my phone.

Was I reading too much into this? Had Mia genuinely been overwhelmed and I was being too arrogant to believe this might be a hard transition for her?

My beautiful, sweet Mia, who sat patiently while her dream-like gaze took in the other shops. This was the kind of life she couldn't have imagined, coming from that impoverished home in Charlotte.

My over analyzing brain had always served me well.

He'd been wearing the cap of Charlotte's football team.

There was one other man who might cause that kind of distress to rise behind Mia's soft blue eyes. The monster who'd shot up a fourteen-year-old Mia with cocaine to silence her, only long enough to overdose her mother and leave her dying on the living room floor. The man I'd had my private investigator hunting down.

Perhaps, I mused darkly, her mother's dealer had come to us.

"Everything okay?" she asked softly.

I smiled her way. "You're mine, so yes."

CHAPTER 12

NOW I UNDERSTOOD those smitten poets and their endless expounding of logic long lost, and others who died willingly for their lovers in war, or peace, or just because, and broken hearted cries from those who announced they'd never recover from losing their one true love.

I no longer cared for the time before her.

It was hard to remember it now. These emotions gripped me too profoundly. How far I'd come in letting go and letting her in.

I wasn't ready to let Mia see I'd developed this chink in my amour. A weakness of sorts. I refused to let her know how she affected me. Didn't need anyone to see this once impenetrable man had fallen hard.

I'd been accused of enjoying watching others burn.

I'd been sorely misunderstood.

It was more about my desire to help others live life to the full, love completely, burn up with a frenzy to devour all the world had to offer. Perhaps my lack of love had been a catalyst to live vicariously through others. I'd pushed Richard, Scarlet, Lotte, and Penny to the brink when it came to finding happiness, all the while holding back on my own.

Though now, I too savored every second of being with a woman whose presence brought me to my knees.

Mia and I hadn't separated since leaving Badgley Mischka.

That look of fear had shaken us both, not least because I

couldn't stand the thought of anyone ever hurting her again.

I took her for a leisurely lunch in the Luxe Rodeo Drive hotel, where we'd ate a light salad and I'd laughed at her silly jokes, so loud we'd drawn unwanted attention from the other diners. It was good to see her relax again.

We returned home to Beverly Hills.

During the afternoon, I'd sat on a lounger in the garden and read that Chuck Palahniuk novel I'd been dying to get to. Finally I relaxed after a grueling few months of working flat out. I sipped on lemon water and frequently glanced up from my Kindle to enjoy the sight of Mia swimming laps.

This is what she did to me. She made me slow down. Gave me a reason to escape from my usual routine of time spent at the office, running Chrysalis, and dabbling in the running of Cole Tea from a safe distance.

In her last life, Mia had been a mermaid. I was sure of it. If there was water, Mia would be drawn to it, whether it was swimming pools, fountains, or taking long, luxurious baths.

She threw me a wave and I waved back.

Having grown up in poverty, she was incapable of taking anything for granted and always experienced what I shared with rapt attention. She was a healthy reminder that grand houses and fast cars were reserved for the rich. Though despite my moneyed upbringing, I'd always been conscious of my privileged life.

Just after my twelfth birthday, Aunt Rose had taken both me and Henry to work in a soup kitchen for a day where we'd delivered hot meals to the homeless. Those memories left a lasting impression. Rose's way of rounding out our education. She was my favorite aunt not least because she was a frequent visitor to our boarding school when we were kids, bringing our favorite sugared treats as well as delivering the kind of affection our mother had failed to realize we needed.

Aunt Rose had served as a nursing officer in the Vietnamese War, and despite marrying into a wealthy family later, she remembered her heritage and taught Henry and I to do the same.

I'd always be grateful to her for that.

Because of Rose's insight, it was easier for me to relate to Mia, and see to her smooth transition into this life. She'd always treated others with respect. I could ask no more from a partner willing to share in my philanthropic pursuits.

I rose from the lounger and joined her by the pool and signaled to her. She swam to the edge, climbed up the pool stairs, and trotted toward me, falling into the large towel I held open for her.

We snuggled on the lounger and napped the rest of the day away.

At sunset, I escorted her upstairs for us to get ready for Scarlet's party.

Mia paused in the doorway when she saw what was waiting for her on the bed. She glanced my way and I gave a knowing nod.

She strolled over and cautiously unwrapped the ribbon off the large Badgley Mischka box.

"Cameron." She reached in and withdrew the dress she'd tried on in the store.

"Ms. Lauren," I said firmly. "Do not refuse me."

She ran her hands over the black material.

I gave a wave of my hand to emphasize it was nothing. "I'm implementing a new level of security. All doors and windows locked. No entry without knowledge of the code."

Her gaze snapped up to hold mine.

Oh yes, my darling, I know.

I didn't push her for answers. No matter how much I wanted to.

"Why?" she said.

"I want you to feel safe."

Her hands traced over the dress again and she held it up.

"You're wearing it tonight."

She tucked a stray hair behind her ear. "I can't accept it—"

"You will."

"Perhaps—"

"Mia."

Her eyelids fluttered in reservation.

I sat on the bed and pulled her toward me, removing the dress from her hands and laying it aside. She didn't need a stern master right now, she needed affection, needed understanding. She straddled me and wrapped her hands around my neck.

I hugged her. "This represents more than a dress. It's me anticipating your needs and fulfilling them."

She buried her face in the crook of my neck.

I leaned back and tipped her chin up. "We must be sensitive to Richard's feelings. If he sees you wearing something he—"

"You're right."

"My parents are visiting tomorrow," I said. "I'm looking forward to them getting to know you better."

She looked nervous.

"It's just dinner."

"They were nice to me last time I met them."

"They're fond of you."

She lowered her gaze shyly.

"I'll be right there beside you."

Yes she was feisty, but God she was so damn vulnerable still. Her past had almost destroyed her.

I'd captured her in that Chrysalis dungeon and used every trick in my arsenal of psychological skills to extract the truth of what had really happened to her at fourteen. Her psyche remained fragile, as did her heart, and I knew without a doubt I was the only man who got her.

"I will protect you until my last breath, Mia. You know that don't you?"

"Yes." Our gazes locked.

"It's imperative you trust me." I wanted to ease her angst. "Whenever you're ready to open up, I'm here."

"It's all so perfect."

"That frightens you?"

"What if it's too perfect? What if something bad happens to ruin it?"

"We in the profession call that pessimism."

She looked endearing. "You're the most important thing in my life."

"Thing?"

"Person. I mean, man."

"Glad we clarified that."

She ran her fingertips over my cheek, her eyes searching my face, finding comfort in what she saw.

I reached low, grabbed the fine strip of material that served as her bikini bottom, and snapped it off.

"It was in the way," I said.

She cupped my face. Her gaze moved downward, watching me free myself.

She surrendered to my kiss, this once feisty sub who fought my command of her.

She bit my lip and the sting made me flinch and pull back.

"Punish me," she whispered.

"But you haven't done anything wrong."

She fell to her knees before me.

"Mia, let's just cuddle."

"Please, I need this."

She kissed the tip of my cock, those endearing lips pouty, her tongue tracing the ridges, flicking and stroking. I'd taught her well. She'd cupped my balls in her mouth in a sensual tease, massaging in a circular motion.

With her head bobbing between my thighs, her mouth brilliantly sucking my hardness, I marveled at this young woman who'd evolved into such a profound lover. I'd fallen into the very trap I'd set for my best friend.

I was spellbound.

This inner war I'd fought to honor my promise to train and return her had been lain waste. My ability to keep Mia at arm's length was an impossible quest. The way I reacted to her sweetness now, even with my cock in her mouth, rendering me the one captured.

"Good girl, Mia."

She lapped around the head, her delicate hands cupping my balls, her feverish mouth tracing along the underside of the base before sucking in her cheeks and drawing me all the way into the back of her throat. Her eyelids closed in ecstasy.

She let out the longest moan of contentment, that vibration of sound encompassing my erection as the sensation burst outward, alighting every nerve, every cell, and I went with it, letting go, willing her to do whatever she wanted.

Playing with locks of her hair, my eyelids grew heavy. My need to be inside her consumed every thought.

I pulled her up, positioned her above me, and pushed into her, all the way, thoughts stolen by the madness of this moment and the need to fill her.

Holding Mia against me I was undone, gripping her against

my chest and raising my hips off the bed to pound her, delighting in the sound of our sex slapping against each other—

We fell over into the abyss together, her rhythmic clenches insistently demanding, and me lost in this sea of pleasure, stilling, absorbing it all, all this intensity, all of her.

I was consumed by this ecstasy tearing through me.

This was what it was to love without barriers.

Bliss.

She collapsed on top of me and we fell back onto the bed, both drifting off like that, with me still inside her.

We stirred in the late afternoon.

Possessively I'd bathed her in the shower, kneeling before her to kiss between her thighs, suckling her there until she'd shuddered against me and screamed my name.

Again.

No matter how many times I took her, it wasn't enough.

I'd dried her off with a soft towel and she let me pamper her.

Beautifully post fucked and naked and newly bathed, she'd lain spread out on the bed, lush golden locks curling around her as she watched me dress.

I chose my usual casual wear of Roberto Cavalli jeans and navy blue shirt and black jacket and dragged a comb through my hair, and then dabbed a splash of Clive Christian cologne on my neck.

I dressed Mia in the new luxury underwear Sylvia Hudson had chosen for her and delivered earlier, under my direction. Savoring the smoothness of her skin, I eased those fine panties up Mia's thighs and secured her bra, cupping her breasts into that exquisite Badgley Mischka dress. I knelt at her feet and assisted her into strappy Louboutins.

She tied up her hair, leaving strands spiraling over her neck, showing off her ruby studded collar. She looked beautiful and she hadn't applied makeup yet.

She disappeared inside the bathroom to do just that.

When she reappeared, she'd transformed her already radiant complexion with a soft blush, and those smoky eyes caught the light. That seductive way she peered beneath long lashes, and her lips were plumped with pink gloss.

Men were going to hate me tonight and women would be in

awe of her.

I tipped a drop of cologne onto my fingertip and traced the edge of the droplet on her throat. I'd marked her with my scent.

"I hate being late," I said.

"We're not late. We'll be right on time."

"No, Mia, we're going to be late."

"Traffic?"

I ran my thumb over her bottom lip.

CHAPTER 13

THE LOCATION CHANGED.

We were no longer headed to The Strand, having been redirected by Shay to Greystone Manor.

Mia sat beside me in the back of the limo looking remarkably fresh, considering I'd tied her to the bedpost and spent the last hour taking her to the edge of pleasure and teasing her into a frenzy.

This addiction wasn't easing, these feelings I'd held back for far too long were all-consuming and showed no promise of letting up.

My fingers traced through her golden locks and I eased a wisp of hair behind her ear. "Apparently a celebrity is having a party at the Strand tonight and the place is crawling with paparazzi."

"Scarlet won't mind?" said Mia.

"No."

We arrived just after 10PM.

Taking my hand, Mia elegantly climbed out of the limo.

We were within full view of the line of guests waiting on the red carpet to enter the club and were cordoned off by a velvet rope. Mia looked stunning and it was no surprise their gazes lingered on her. Her natural flair leant itself to an exquisite style, all flowing locks and fresh faced smile, emanating innocence. Protectively, I wrapped my arm around her.

The stocky bouncer narrowed his gaze when he saw us approaching. He spoke into his headset and gestured we could bypass the line and go on in.

The air-conditioning hit us as we entered the low lit foyer.

As did the music—the base vibrated from the rustic floorboards, alighting an already intense party atmosphere. Young, eager faces fell on us, the men checking Mia out and the women assessing the competition.

The female concierge hurried forward to greet us and in a flurry of caffeine fuelled enthusiasm led us to our party. As usual, Shay had smoothed the way for us. I was always grateful for his attention to detail.

The place was buzzing.

We dodged the stray dancers and hurried along, hoping there were no stragglers from the paparazzi here.

The manor was famed for its vintage style and modern décor, including a large performance stage flooded in bright multicolored lighting, with an outside arcade, and for those like us who needed a more exclusive experience sat the VIP room.

Cheers rose from our friends when we entered the private roped off section. Champagne already flowed and it was good to see Richard, Shay, and Arianna already having a great time. From their flushed faces, they'd hit the dance floor hard. Scarlet, Lotte, and Penny also greeted us warmly with hugs. Penny's husband Miles had also joined us—a soft spoken man who worked as a set designer at Warner Brothers. His calm temperament suited Penny's boisterous nature. He shook my hand and I introduced him to Mia.

"Happy Birthday, Scarlet." I hugged her.

"I'm so happy you're here," she said brightly.

She looked so cute, a far cry from her status of being one of L.A.'s most preeminent dominatrixes, with her flowing auburn locks and elegant black chiffon dress.

We all settled on the leather seats and conversations picked back up.

I leaned back, stretching my arms along the length of the seat, and Mia snuggled beside me. That slow steady beat of music was easy to fall into. The entire place was conducive to people watching. Here and there puffs of smoke escaped from electronic cigarettes, vapor spiraling up and into nothing.

We had a sprawling view of the club. Beyoncé flooded the room with her lyrics about betrayal and heartache, echoing down on hundreds of dancers.

Arianna grabbed Mia's hand and pulled her toward the dance floor. Mia turned to see if I approved and, with a wave, I sent her off to have fun.

It dawned on me I'd never seen her dance.

I savored these firsts with her, keeping my gaze locked on them all the way to the dance floor.

My phone vibrated in my pocket and I pulled it out. My gaze rose to meet Shay's.

He'd sent the text. *I have one of my people on the dance floor.*

I gave a crooked smile.

Shay gave one back.

Mia would no doubt soon disappear into the sea of bodies.

She and Arianna moved perfectly with the base, their hips swaying, both of them mirroring each other. I scanned the crowd for Shay's man but couldn't see him. A pretty woman with an ebony complexion danced rhythmically beneath the lights. She'd closed in on the girls and frequently glanced their way.

Shay called over. "Ex-special forces. Emma kicks ass."

"Good to know," I said. "Don't let her kick mine."

He chuckled.

Mia ignored those around her. Her flushed face and big grin proved she really was enjoying herself.

It was good to see her let herself go.

My thoughts drifted to the first time I'd ever seen her. A screenshot on Tara's phone, my then secretary at Enthrall. Tara had been dating Bailey, Mia's best friend, and she'd fallen head over heels for her. Tara had told me the blonde in the photo was Mia Lauren and she'd been friends with Bailey a long time. I'd taken the liberty of scrolling through Tara's photos, checking out the others. One had stood out. And it had been life changing.

Mia didn't know I'd seen it.

It was of her, Bailey, and Tara, standing on a balcony with their backs facing the camera, all three of them flirtatiously raising their skirts high above their butts. Mia had been the only one wearing panties, but her thong hid nothing. Mia's flirty tilt of her head matched with her innocent smile as she looked back at the camera, her blue eyes sparkling with joy, her beauty enthralling—

Making me catch my breath.

That moment had spurred a need to protect her. Tell her to cover up so some young stud didn't take advantage. Considering I ran one of the most hedonistic club's in the world, it was quite a revelation.

That glorious vision of her in the photo had inspired an idea. One that had come back to haunt me. If I'd failed at one thing in my recruitment of that fresh faced beauty, it was to assume such exhibitionism hadn't come from a virgin.

My one regret with Mia was I'd not been the one to deflower her.

Still, I was more than making up for time with her now. My hands twitched, needing to touch her.

From the dance floor, she gestured she wanted me to join her.

I gestured with a shake of my head, *no*.

The music was loud, and though I managed to hold a conversation with Scarlet, if not a compromised one, it was good to catch up. Had I chosen the venue it would have been an intimate restaurant in Malibu overlooking the ocean. These clubs weren't exactly conducive to fine conversation. But then again that was the point.

I took the chance to talk with everyone and hear their news, savoring these precious hours. Mia and Arianna spent the evening dancing away, their hairstyles now mussed up and their faces blushing wildly.

My phone vibrated again and I glanced down at the message.

Alert for: Dr. Cole, it began, *01:48. Cedars ER. Requests response.*

I texted back: *Dr. C.R. Cole, not on call. Alert A. Feinstein.*

I tucked my phone back and listened into Scarlet and Lotte discussing Lotte's brother's timeshare in Hawaii and plotting their next vacation.

Shay sat beside me and leaned in to speak over the music. "We got the footage you asked for of Rodeo Drive. Wanna tell me what's up?"

"I think Mia saw someone from her past," I said.

"Who?"

"Didn't ask."

He looked surprised.

"If it's who I think, the man left an indelible mark and not in a good way. She didn't mention it, which brings me to the conclusion she suppressed her fear. It's a delicate issue."

"Want me to ask her?"

"No."

"I'll have that black Kia driver's info for you by morning," he said. "My guy's out of the office. He'll run the plates first thing."

"I appreciate that."

Richard leaned over and gave my back a pat. "Got a second?"

"Of course."

We nudged up to a more private corner and huddled close. Richard leaned in to talk more privately. "You look good."

"You too. How are you?"

He stared off at the dance floor.

"You know I love you, right?"

He seemed to think about this for a while. "We miss you at Enthrall."

"We?"

"Me."

"Well that's good."

"I'm having a party at my place next weekend. Shay, Henry, you, and me."

"You're on."

He sat back. "When was the last time you checked your shares?"

"I don't know. A week."

"Tripled."

The air left the room.

The dancers disappeared, everything disappeared.

"Richard, that would make you—"

"A stockbroking genius."

On paper, I was three times the man I was yesterday. He'd pulled off a miracle. My brain tried to catch up. "How?"

"An 8 percent NASDAQ surge." He shrugged. "This month saw the highest number of monthly buyback announcements in history."

And on he went, relaying just how he'd taken my investments and made me three times the money I'd entrusted to him.

My thoughts reeled. "How can I repay you?"

"Steak dinner."

And of course he'd also made a nice commission, adding a few million to his portfolio too, but he deserved every cent.

"I'm at a loss for words." I shrugged out of my jacket, the heat getting to me.

"You had faith in me, Cam." He let a moment sit between us. "That's reward enough."

After Richard's dad had brought down Wall Street, Richard had lost every last one of his clients. Except me.

"What can I tell you, Cam? It's in my blood."

"I'm stunned."

"Maybe now you'll let me dance with your girlfriend?"

I shook my head, feigning the ridiculousness of him asking.

"Go have fun," I said. "Thanks again, Richard. I really appreciate what you've done."

Richard's gaze found Mia in the swarm. "She looks happy." He pushed to his feet and headed over.

My phone vibrated again.

Mia and Arianna greeted Richard warmly, and Mia peered through the crowd and signaled for me to join them.

Scarlet scooted over closer. "How's Richard doing?"

"Good."

"Looks like he still has a thing for her," she said softly.

Too softly, but I'd read her lips.

Richard danced close to Mia, their comfort with being close to each other evident by the way they moved well together with the rhythm of old friends. Mia flashed an uneasy glance my way. I grinned back.

I ran through what might be an appropriate reaction should Richard grind against her, which he was very close to doing. But I took into consideration I'd stolen her from him and he'd just added a few million to my portfolio.

Reaching into my pocket, I pulled out the gift card and handed it Scarlet. "Happy birthday."

She turned it over. "Cameron, it's too much."

"It's your favorite spa. Now you can get pampered every week, like you deserve."

"For the rest of my life," she said, amused. "Cameron, thank you."

"It's from Mia too." I pulled my phone out of my pocket.

Alert for: Dr. Cole, it repeated, *02:37. Cedars ER. Response requested by Dr. Tavon Pierre. Surgical. Urgent.*

Mia, Arianna, and Richard were swallowed up by the crowd.

I gestured to Shay I had to take this. "Tell Mia I'll be right back."

Pushing my way through the throng, I eventually made it to the foyer. Not wanting to have the caller hear me in a nightclub, I stepped outside.

Cold night air hit me with a bitter chill and only then did I realize I'd left my jacket behind. A few more steps and I lingered beside the deserted valet kiosk.

I brought my phone to my ear. "Dr. Cole."

"Dr. Cole," said the familiar chirpy voice of Nurse Saunders. "Sorry to bother you so late, it's Payton. I know you're not on call, but Dr. Pierre needs to talk to you urgently."

"Do you know what the issue is?"

"No, but Dr. Pierre told me to tell you it's urgent."

"Thanks, Payton. How are you?"

"Crazy busy. Just got a multiple MVA. We're slammed."

"Hang in there."

"Hope I didn't wake you?"

"Not at all."

"I'll put you through to Dr. Pierre. Hold on."

"Who's that?" came that familiar timid voice behind me.

I spun round and saw Mia. "Cedars."

"You're not on call."

"No."

"We were just dancing, Cameron," she said.

I narrowed my gaze.

"I love you," she said, her gait unsteady. "You're the most important man in my life. I only want you."

I studied her pupils. "How much have you had to drink?"

"That's not exactly a romantic response."

"How much?"

"Maybe I had a shot."

"Of what?"

"Tequila."

"Arianna bought you a shot?"

"Richard did." She lowered her gaze "He bought one for you.

91

But you'd left. Are you upset with me?"

Running my hand through my hair, along with an appropriate response through my brain, I tried to think of the best way to handle this.

"This is hard for me too," she said.

"Mia, I received a text from Cedars requesting me to call. I stepped out so I could hear."

"Who's Payton?"

"A registered nurse. She was asked to text me by another staff member." I gestured to the building. "My jacket's in there. I'm coming back."

"You gave me permission to dance."

"Cole!" boomed a voice through the phone.

"Tavon?" I raised a hand for Mia to be quiet.

"I'm worried about Richard," Mia whispered.

"One second." Resting my forefinger on my lips, I again insisted she was quiet. "Hey Tavon, everything okay?"

"Yeah, I need to talk to you," he said. "Can't say too much on the phone. When are you in next?"

"How about my office?"

"I need to see you sooner."

Mia rested her hands on her hips. My thoughts drifted to Richard and I wondered what kind of conversation they'd just had. Heartbreak and booze were a dangerous mix.

"Cole?" said Tavon. "You there?"

His voice sounded raw.

I needed to focus. Walking away from Mia, I stood beneath the green awning. "I'm listening."

"I think I'm having a panic attack."

"What caused it?"

"Lost a patient."

"What are your symptoms?"

"I still have his blood on my sleeve."

A wave of dread. "From a procedure?"

"Yes."

"Where are you, Tavon?"

"ICU."

"Your symptoms?"

"I feel like shit."

Mia neared me, smiling broadly, and poked my stomach to get my attention.

I held my hand over the phone. "Mia, this is important."

She froze, her eyes wide. "Do you still love me?" she slurred.

I reached for her, spun her around, and cupped my hand over her mouth playfully, pulling her back to my chest and holding her tight to control her.

She wiggled in my arms and brushed against my groin.

"How quickly can you get here?" asked Tavon.

"I'm just down the road. I'm on my way. Change out of those scrubs."

"Okay."

Mia stilled and let out a soft sigh of her arousal. It vibrated against my palm.

"Tavon," I said, "head to the cafeteria and get some tea. Watch the TV. Do not call or text anyone. Talk to no one. I'm on my way."

"Did I wake you?" he said.

"No. Make it decaf."

"I really appreciate this."

"See you soon." I hung up and released Mia.

She spun round and stared up at me.

"Mia, I have to go."

"No!"

Of course the last time a girlfriend had made a scene during a party I'd dumped her soon after. That girlfriend had been McKenzie, and she'd thrown a fit because I'd gotten called into work.

I tipped Mia's chin up. "This is important."

"Sorry," she said sheepishly. "I'll get your jacket."

I grabbed her wrist. "There's no time."

She tried to wriggle free. "But you'll get cold."

I pulled the phone back to my ear. "Leo, bring the car round."

"Let go of her!" A raspy voice—

The woman wore all black. The forty-something vixen wore a skirt too short and hoop earrings too big and looked spaced out. She was high. The question was from what?

She teetered on high heels.

"Mia's my girlfriend," I reassured her. "She's fine."

"Doesn't look fine," she snapped.

"He has to go," Mia told her. "Something happened."

"Please be quiet," I muttered and hugged Mia.

"What the fuck," said the woman. "Let her go. She doesn't wanna go with you."

I let Mia go and stepped back, hoping to deflate the tension. I reached for my phone and texted Shay: *Bring jacket. Mia's bag. Fast.*

I peered up to see the woman glaring.

"Just texting my buddy," I said calmly. "Letting him know where we are."

"I'm fine," said Mia to the woman. "Really, he's my boyfriend."

"He had his hand over your mouth," she said. "Didn't look fine."

Fucking great, I caressed my brow to lessen this impending headache.

The woman grabbed Mia's arm. "Come stand with us." She gestured to her friends.

Mia tried to twist out of the woman's grip. "I don't want to."

I wrapped my fingers around the woman's hand and pried off her fingers. "You're scaring my girlfriend. Please let her go."

The limo pulled around and I breathed a sigh of relief.

Pain—

Sharp—

My head jolted back.

Agony in my lip, resonating across my face.

Stunned.

Disorientated, I raised my hands to defend myself from the second punch heading fast toward me, a tattooed fist that had almost knocked me out with the first strike.

A blur of movement.

My attacker now lay flat on his back.

I blinked at the sight of Emma and her Ronda Rousey moves. A slow motion vision of her now slid between Mia and that woman. Mia stumbled back into my arms. I caught her and hugged her into me possessively.

Both our attackers now lay on the ground, moans rising. Emma calmly leaned over them, her expression pure matter-of-fact. Her demeanor all business as usual.

Shay marched toward us carrying my jacket and Mia's handbag.

Emma, his hardcore guard, gave him a look of triumph.

"Get Cole in the car," he yelled.

CHAPTER 14

WHAT THE HELL.

Our limo shot away from the curb, pushing us back in our seats.

I pressed ice cubes wrapped in a handkerchief to my lower lip. It stung. Every nerve, sinew, and cell was on high alert.

I wanted to go back and punch someone.

"Sure you're okay, Mia?" I lowered the handkerchief and examined her arm, checking for contusions.

"I'm fine." She reached for my hand and placed the cold pack back on my mouth. "I'm so sorry."

My forced smile of reassurance made me wince. "They attacked us. They were drunk. Or high. Or both."

Shay handed Mia an icepack from the first aid kit and she replaced it with the rudimentary one he'd made from the wine cooler and pressed it to my mouth. The cold burned.

"Fuck," I mumbled. "My parents fly in tomorrow."

Mia looked horrified. "Can you tell them you tripped?"

Shay scoffed as he texted. "Let's hope your attackers don't know who you are."

"I imagine it ended up recorded on a few phones," I said.

Shay glanced up. "Data is currently being deleted."

"You can do that?" asked Mia.

Shay looked over at me. "My specialty."

"The White House tried to poach him," I said. "Offered quite the salary."

"D.C.'s too cold," he said, and feigned being chilled to the bone.

I eased the icepack off my lip and cringed when I saw blood.

"Cameron told me he'd pay danger pay." Shay winked at Mia.

"Talking of which—" I gestured to Shay's phone— "how are they?"

"Dazed, but fine. Emma usually just stuns her victims. She can do a lot worse."

"Very enthusiastic employee," I said dryly.

"I like her." He tucked his smartphone away. "He could have had a gun, Cameron."

I shrugged. "Give them medical attention. Whatever's needed."

"I'm handling it." Shay's phone buzzed and he read the screen. "Emma says they're from out of town so we may just be in luck."

"They can't sue us," said Mia. "They attacked us."

"Press charges," said Shay.

"My aversion to the press won't let that happen," I said. "Let's put it behind us."

"What's going on at Cedars?" asked Shay.

"I have a colleague who had a difficult case."

"It can't wait till tomorrow?"

I gave a shake of my head. "I'll send Scarlet flowers."

Scarlet would understand, she always did. In fact everyone in my life was used to my frequent exits, and right now Mia also seemed to be handling it well.

Seeing her in danger had triggered a desire to do whatever it took to protect her at any cost.

Within ten minutes, the towers of Cedars Sinai loomed.

"Shay, take Mia home," I said. "Stay with her. I won't be long."

"Sure."

"I can't come with you?"

"I won't be long."

She looked uncertain.

I let out a long sigh. "The first time you lose a patient you don't think you'll ever be able to breathe again. Doctors grieve, despite the emotion being taboo."

"Have you ever lost a patient?"

I held her gaze.

She took my hand. "Can we do anything?"

"Get some rest. I'll be home soon."

The car dropped me off outside the ER.

Comfortable with leaving Shay to watch over Mia, I headed on through the sliding doors and a stale warmth hit me. The waiting room was half full, the faces of the patients a mixture of frustration and boredom.

I withdrew my ID from my wallet and security let me through.

The place bustled with its usual frenetic energy, a mixture of organized chaos and tension. In the middle of this controlled storm, I lingered at an unused console and shook the mouse to awaken the computer screen, tapping in my code to access the system.

With a few taps, Tavon's schedule over the last five days came up.

I entered his last patient file, which ended with a time of death. Mr. Ray Arnold had been admitted into the morgue.

I went back to read Tavon's pre-op notes. He'd yet to document his report post-procedure, so I moved on to the OR nurse's detailed narration, and then the anesthesiologists.

The surrounding mayhem continued around me.

In a flurry of brunette locks, Payton gave my arm a tap. Her brightness was a nice distraction from the data I'd been engrossed in. She held an IV bag of potassium. Other than a chipped fingernail, she looked perfectly groomed for this time of the morning, and even her lipstick was holding up.

"Did you get to speak with Tavon?" Her southern accent was strong, her breathless tone revealing.

"I did, thank you, Payton. How are things here?"

"Better. Did you get into a fight?"

"You should see the other guy."

"I don't doubt it."

"Only a few more hours and shift's over."

"Thank goodness."

"Planning anything nice?"

She lowered her gaze. "I was meeting a friend but something came up."

"His loss."

She narrowed her gaze. "Who says it's a guy?"

"Perhaps a spa day is on the cards. Time to rejuvenate."

She blinked at me as though the idea hadn't crossed her mind. "Maybe I will." She glanced over toward the computer screen.

I'd already exited the file. The Cedars logo came back on view.

Her phone buzzed. "Gotta go."

She scurried off down the corridor, her long lean frame attracting looks from a few other staff, but she seemed oblivious.

I headed on out, avoiding patients pushed in wheelchairs or on gurneys, staff hurrying by, and I nodded to a few who I recognized.

The pungent scent of bleach faded as I stepped out of the building and headed across the street, making the short distance to the south tower.

From chaos to calm. The Cedars cafeteria was deserted.

I perused the line of cereals and went for two bowls of oatmeal. Joining them on my tray were two fresh paper cups of decaf breakfast tea. I paid for the food at checkout and headed on farther back into the generous seating area. There were numerous tables and chairs and quite a few preferable red booths.

A handful of night staff were taking their breaks, most of them spaced out and counting down to hitting the sack. A few stared up at the walled TV screen, an anchor on CNN spewing the latest doom and gloom.

Tavon sat in the far right corner.

His deep brown eyes inherited from African American parents exuded kindness. Those rugged good looks were forged from years of putting medicine first. His stubble matched my own.

"Hey there," I said, placing the tray on the table between us and easing into his private booth.

"Dr. Cole," he said. "Thank you for being here."

"Cameron," I said. "Of course."

His gaze lowered to my mouth. "What happened to you?"

"All part of the therapeutic process to let you see I too am human."

"Seriously, what happened?"

"A misunderstanding."

His frown deepened. "And I thought I had a rough night."

"How are things at home?"

"Good. This conversation—"

"Strictly confidential."

"I appreciate that."

I lifted the bowl of oatmeal toward him and took one for myself. Same with the tea. "So, what's up?"

He scratched the back of his neck. "There's the usual strains. You know, long hours, taking a little more time these days to shake off the day when I get home."

"How did the affair start?" I ate a spoonful of oatmeal.

"Excuse me?"

"With Payton?"

He stared at me for a long time. "You spoke with her?"

"Bumped into her when I came through the ER."

"She told you about us?"

"No, you just did."

He looked perplexed. "It's nothing."

"I'm afraid Payton doesn't feel that way."

He jolted upright. "You sure you didn't—"

"Talk to her about your affair? No, I merely picked up her tone of affection when she spoke your name. You didn't tell her why you'd called me?"

"I don't need her to know—"

"She's your professional equal."

"This has nothing to do with what happened in the OR."

"I believe you."

"Then why bring it up?"

I shrugged. "An observation. It's what I do. I'm assuming that's why I'm here."

"You do have a reputation for seeing beyond the ordinary."

I feigned surprise.

"Um, well this is awkward," he said.

"Not as awkward as why I'm here." I took another bite of oatmeal. "This is good."

He blinked at me, his face full of doubt.

I'd knocked Tavon even more off balance.

Cruel, but necessary.

He sat back, his face worn with worry. "The Septal Myectomy

was going great, vitals were stable, the—"

"You have to try this—" I pointed with my spoon. "Delicious."

He blinked down at the pot. "Kind of lost my appetite."

"Humor me. Try it."

He scooped a mouthful of creamy oatmeal with his plastic spoon and nodded in appreciation. His lowered eyelids revealed he really was hungry.

As Tavon ran through what happened in-between mouthfuls, I made a mental run through of what I knew about this procedure. It was complicated and risky, requiring the patient to be placed on cardiopulmonary bypass for up to six hours. The technique was so delicate it could only be conducted by a skilled surgeon on a still heart.

He didn't need to know I'd reviewed the minute by minute documentation of the surgery, and with each word he spoke I checked off my review of his case.

"No one would have known how affected I was," he said. "I just left ICU and went right to the coffee room. Asked Payton to text you."

"I see."

He rested his hand on his chest. "I have this sense of doom. Can't shake it. It's really bad."

"The fact you called a psychiatrist and not a therapist reflects self-awareness." I took a sip of tea. "To a degree."

"How do you mean?"

"Your diagnosis."

"Excuse me?"

"How long have we known each other?"

"Three years."

"I've been meaning to break it to you and now's a good a time as any."

He looked surprised.

"It's quite clear to me you're a psychopath." I gestured to his drink. "Try the tea. It's refreshing."

He stared at me, waiting for the punch line.

I nudged the cereal to the side and patted my pockets. "My pad's in my office. I'll call you in a prescription."

"Not funny, Cameron."

"From what I've seen so far, you really are worthy of this classification of personality disorder."

"Psychopaths show no remorse. They lack empathy, they…"

"Exactly."

He frowned, as though mulling it over. "What is this?"

I gestured to my mouth. "The reason I got punched was because I was outside taking your call and someone attacked my girlfriend. She's fine by the way, considering—" I raised my hand. "Not that you care. Being a psychopath."

His gaze swept the cafeteria warily.

"There's a line of therapy we can proceed with—"

"I have feelings," he said. "I have guilt over Payton—"

"That's fear of getting caught."

"Still, it's an emotion."

"It's merely a reflex of concern that you won't be able to continue fucking her."

He glared at me.

"Your diagnosis is a hard pill to swallow." I resisted cringing at that choice of words.

"Now listen, I'm a good surgeon. No, great surgeon. I've dedicated my life to medicine. Obsessed over getting it right. And yes, I screwed up but how many more lives have I saved?"

"So what you're essentially saying is losing a patient happens from time to time?"

"Yes."

"And sometimes we get it wrong?" I raised my spoon. "Not that I'm saying you did."

He turned his hands over. They'd stopped shaking. Tavon's face was marred with confusion.

He was young. Brilliant. And a great surgeon.

I had to push him over the edge so he'd be relieved when he came back to firmer ground. I needed to anchor him to a sense of safety. Get him to trust his own judgment again.

"When was the last time you ate?" I said.

"Five, yesterday."

"The surgery started at four fifteen and went on for six hours. You stayed in intensive care for a further two hours trying to save your patient. You didn't leave his side."

"You read my report?"

"Yes."

He looked thoughtful. "I had lunch. A snack before surgery."

"You were fine during the surgery. Performed every incision flawlessly. After leaving the ICU, you spiraled. Became hypoglycemic. You need to eat. This—" I pointed to the oatmeal – "will return your blood sugar to normal."

"I do feel a little better."

"Let Payton meet a nice single man. One who will take care of her the way she takes care of her patients. No more cheating on your wife."

"As if it's any of your business."

"Why did you marry Lynette?" I asked. "After all, she was the most incredible woman you'd ever met."

He frowned at me.

I added, "You're an egotistical bastard who wouldn't have settled for less."

He gave a look of relent. "Do you talk to all your patients like this?"

"You're not my patient," I said. "You don't need therapy. You need to grow a pair."

He rolled his eyes. "Psychopath? Was that the best you could think of?"

I arched a brow. "You're off the reservation. Thought I'd join you. See what it feels like in the cheap seats."

He let out a laugh. "Are you like this all the time?"

"Feel better?"

Tavon caressed his brow. "Fuck you."

"I take it that's a yes."

"It's a fuck you."

"You're smiling again."

"This is the quiet rage of a psychopath."

"Nice."

"And I thought I was messed up."

"You're welcome," I said. "You're grieving for your patient. He reminded you of your dad. Your father was a great surgeon too, apparently. A lot to live up to. You're setting the bar impossibly high."

"And how this is relevant?"

"Your patient was the same age as your dad when he died."

"You accessed my father's records?"

"Yes."

"How did you know he died here?"

"I checked his name. He came up in MedRecs."

He swallowed hard. A wave of emotion.

"I figured you'd have him in the best hospital," I said.

"That was a year ago."

"We don't get the privilege of ruminating. There's another life waiting to be saved."

"I lost sight of it."

"Tavon," I said. "You've been up for twenty-four hours straight. Give yourself a break. Go home. Make love to your wife and get some sleep."

"Sorry about your girlfriend."

I smiled at his thoughtfulness. "I let my guard down."

"Thank you for seeing me."

"I was here for the oatmeal," I said. "Thanks for having breakfast with me."

He looked sheepish. "I didn't know who else would understand."

"My door's always open."

"Not sure I like your brand of therapy, Dr. Cole."

"We're not so dissimilar, Dr. Pierre."

"What? We're both arrogant fucks but we get the job done?"

"We do."

He shook his head, his wariness lifting and the brightness returning.

"Your patient died of heart disease," I said. "Nothing you could have done would have saved him."

Tavon sat back and his shoulders lowered.

I took a sip of tea. "Before the operation, your patient stared into your eyes pleading for you to save his life."

"They always do."

"He asked for your best, Tavon. You gave it."

His lips trembled. "A more experienced surgeon—"

"Might not have fought so hard. He or she might have seen such a diseased heart and not spent nine hours trying to do the impossible."

"I was so close."

"Grief is not just about our pain. It's about honoring our patient's memory and expressing our belief that each life has meaning. That Mr. Ray Arnold counted." I raised my cup. "To Mr. Arnold and the indelible mark he left on this world."

Tavon raised his cup and knocked it against mine.

"What is it about tea that always makes you feel better?" he said.

"Theanine. It increases the brain's production of GABA. Meditation has the same effect."

Tea, a five thousand year-old beverage that had made my family a fortune over generations. It had always been more about the art of tea, the healing properties, the ability to soothe that had fascinated me. A sense of pride that my ancestors had been the ones who'd brought tea to the masses. A legacy that included our continued links with India.

Tavon had no idea I was the son of a billionaire tea mogul. In fact, most people didn't and there was no reason for them to. It served no purpose and threatened to blur the lines of friendship.

"Will you stay with me a while?" he said softly.

"Of course." I offered a reassuring smile. "I'll get us some more tea."

CHAPTER 15

LIGHT SHIMMERED OFF the few golden locks appearing above the covers. Those fine strands were like burnished gold.

Mia clutched one of my shirts. She ached for me too.

My sweet, sweet lover, slept soundly, burrowed safely in our bed.

Lingering at the end, I realized how much I needed her. Mia's sweetness lifted this burden of knowledge that weighed all too heavily. The cruelty of life's sting slipped away when she was with me, even with her asleep.

If this was what it meant to be the moth, I didn't care. I yearned to burn up in her.

Be inside her.

I stripped off my clothes and kicked off my shoes and it felt symbolic, as though I was removing the residue of these last few hours. That incident at the club, where I'd realized Mia's vulnerability and knew what I was capable of to protect her.

The strain of seeing Tavon's pain and soothing him the best way I knew. Not with words of sympathy, but relighting that fierceness within him, that desire to forge on bravely despite truly comprehending the fragility of the lives we held in our hands.

Outside that window, dawn loomed. The world could go on alone.

The serenest retreat awaited me.

Mia, my refuge, my escape.

Upon the side table rested *The Hero with a Thousand Faces* by Joseph Campbell. Mia had found the book in my library and brought it up here to read.

Lifting the end of the comforter, I slipped under it and made my way, planting kisses to her feet and moving upward. She stirred and shuddered when my tongue met her sex. I lapped and flicked her clit, selfishly needing her.

"You're home," she said sleepily. "I'm so happy."

I replied by kissing deeper, taking her there firmly, lavishing more affection, tasting that which I'd become addicted to, bestowing suckles until she arched her back and breathed in gasps of pleasure.

"Not yet, Mia," I whispered.

"Oh, please."

No one could give her what she needed like me. I was the only man who could truly love her the way she deserved. I'd worship her every day like this.

I rose over her and grabbed her wrists, pinning her arms above her head and to the mattress before thrusting deep inside, feeling her tautness, her wetness allowing for my slow, leisurely glide.

I stared down at this impossible conquest.

"Please," she begged.

"Not yet."

"I can't..."

"You can and you will."

Slower thrusts, deep and powerful, her body trembling beneath me.

"I'm going to die from pleasure," she stuttered.

I buried my face in her neck to hide my smile.

"Now?" she said.

"No." I rubbed my pelvis against her sex with each glide.

"Oh God."

"Obey."

"Yes, sir."

I gave her this nice and slow fucking she deserved. I withdrew all the way out, followed by a long steady thrust. Holding off, holding her back, I kept her lingering on the edge and moved slower still when she neared.

On and on, until her moans echoed around us.

Her eyelids grew heavy, and there was a sprinkle of moisture on her upper lip. Her stare glazed with concentration as she tried to obey.

This slow torture of pleasure made my cock ache for release, yet seeing her obey and restrain from climaxing intensified my own mind-blowing orgasm that I could no longer hold back.

"You may come."

Her cries fractured the silence. Her body went rigid in ecstasy and her orgasm took her over. Eyes closed, she shuddered. Her rare mixture of innocence and passion was impossible not to crave.

My meaning to life.

I followed her over into the abyss and the world disappeared around us. Nothing mattered, only her. We lay like this for a while, me above her staring down into her eyes.

I collapsed beside her, all drama having dissipated from my mind like a foggy memory

"Good morning," she said at last.

"Good morning."

"That's kind of a cool alarm clock you've got going on there."

"Have you reduced me to a technological device?"

"That's the most amazing way to wake up." She threw herself onto my chest and rested her head against my heart. "How's your friend?"

"Doing better."

"I can't imagine what it must be like. All that responsibility."

I raised my head to look at her. "Tavon will be fine."

"Amazing how one person dedicates their life to saving others and other people out there think nothing of taking lives."

"My little philosopher."

Her breathing softened and she fell back to sleep.

Despite wanting to savor every second with her, sleep could have me for now. Exhaustion dragged me down.

Dreams rolled through until there was nothing.

"Cameron."

Birdsong rose from outside the window.

I blinked awake.

"Cameron?" Mia said again.

I reached for her. "Get back in."

"I can't."

I raised my head to look at her.

She'd dressed in one of the floral Elie Tahari dresses I'd bought for her. I knew how much she loved that designer and it made me happy she'd chosen a Sunday morning to wear it. She looked gorgeous, her outfit flawless, her hair golden curls of perfection.

I reached for her.

She jumped back. "I have to entertain your parents."

"They don't fly in until six." I glanced at the bedside clock. "What's the time?"

"Eleven."

It was still morning, at least.

"They moved their trip up," she said.

I scrambled for my phone and read the texts, all of them from my mom.

I shot up. "They're here?"

"They kind of are."

"What does kind of mean?"

"That's my way of breaking it to you slowly they're here."

I scrambled out of bed. "At the front door?"

"No, inside. Well outside now. I've been chatting with them. I've gotten them settled in the garden. I made tea and croissants."

Frozen to the spot, I stared at her. "How long have they been here?"

"Couple of hours."

"And you didn't wake me?"

"I wanted to, but after I told your mom you'd had a late night at the hospital she wanted to let you sleep in."

The thought of Mia being left alone with my parents without my deflecting the conversation made me inwardly cringe. There was no doubt my parents would take full advantage of Mia's sweetness to inquire about my life. As well as ask questions about us.

Mia was wearing the pumps I'd bought her. My gaze quickly broke from that hummingbird tattoo on her ankle.

"You look pretty." I hopped into my PJs. "What's been the general gist of the conversation?"

"Maybe you should put pants on?"

I blinked at her, the heaviness of sleep lingering. "I should shower."

"Do you want to borrow some of my makeup?"

I traced my fingers along my lower lip. "No, but thank you for the offer."

She turned to go. "I'll keep them entertained."

"Good, yes, that's one plan."

Mia paused by the door and faced me. "Don't worry, Cameron. I survived the 'which university did you attend,' question from your dad."

I merely arched my brows in interest despite my heart rate taking off. "What did you tell them?"

"The truth. That I'm your sex slave and was initially hired at Enthrall—"

"Not funny."

She grinned. "I'm more than capable of protecting you."

"There was no mention of Chrysalis?"

"No, but I did sign your mom up for a session at Enthrall."

"Humor's not your strong point." My blood pressure spiked and my head felt twice the size. "Where are my PJs?"

"You're wearing them."

"I know that." I bit the inside of my cheek.

"Can I get you anything?"

"A time machine."

She gave a salute. "I'm on it, boss."

"I'll be right out." I headed into the bathroom.

My reflection in the mirror made me flinch. That late night didn't look good on me, even if my bruised lip was less swollen. The cut healed, but I still looked like I'd been in a fight. I ran through all the explanations that might get me off the hook and they all led back to idiocy.

Standing under the faucet, I woke up further beneath the pounding hot water. It felt good and eased my headache. Mia really was beautiful and I couldn't be prouder to show her off, but my mother's interrogation might very well break her. They'd be the kind of questions that came laden with judgment. I wasn't sure Mia was ready for that level of inquiry from my mom on a mission. Though surprisingly, Mia hadn't appeared too shaken from having hosted without me so far.

Having navigated time spent with my parents with the

precision of a Cold War diplomat, I felt a dreadful loss of control that my father would have been provided unfettered access to all aspects of my life through Mia, and without me policing the content. After running through several scenarios for damage control, I got out the shower, wrapped a towel around my waist, and made my way back into the bedroom.

Not having gone for my morning run was throwing me off.

Mia was gone.

My throat tightened when I realized she'd disobeyed and returned to my parents. Yes, I might be considered a deviant rogue, but lately I'd been pulling back on my high wire kink. I hadn't visited Chrysalis in days. This woman was changing me. And I'd changed her, giving her the confidence to navigate life's tricky paths.

I dressed in black slacks, a white shirt, and even went out of my way to wear a tie. A little formal for a Sunday, but no doubt my parents would be elegantly dressed and they might even add my lack of jacket to the list of criticisms they'd chastise me about later.

The damage was done, and Mia returning to spend time with my parents wasn't going to reverse the fallout. I almost forgave her for not waking me when I saw the mug of coffee and a bottle of Advil she'd placed on the bedside table.

Those tablets and that coffee were my consolatory prize for the equivalent of experiencing the seven levels of Dante's Inferno, and upon reflection Dante had been writing about having brunch with my parents.

Several gulps later and mug in hand, I made my way down.

The cool morning breeze hit me as I stepped outside.

A stray leaf floated on the surface of the swimming pool and I peered up with an accusatory glare at the tree, wondering if my dad had caught nature's faux pas. The garden was perfect other than that.

To my surprise, my parents appeared to be happily chatting away with Mia at a poolside table. I braced myself for *that* look.

Instead, I was greeted by Mom's unusual chirpy demeanor and my dad's seeming calmness. Mom looked flawless in pink Chanel and Dad's dark suit oozed formal. I was underdressed.

"Mia should have woken me," I said by way of apology.

"Nonsense," said Mom. "Mia explained you'd spent the early hours at the hospital. We're glad you caught up on your sleep."

"What happened to you?" Dad rose to greet me.

"It's nothing," I said, circling the table to kiss my mom on the cheek.

"Doesn't look like nothing," he said.

"Can I get you anything?" I patted his back affectionately when he hugged me.

I was almost thrown by the way his hold lingered.

He gestured to the table. "We have everything we need."

Mia had placed a silver tray on the table and on it sat a tea urn. Another tray held a porcelain plate laden with croissants. China plates rested on each placemat with merely croissant crumbs as evidence of a breakfast enjoyed. Mia's remained uneaten. There was even a butter dish and the appropriate knives.

"This looks nice," I said, winking at Mia.

She bustled with pride. "Have one."

"I think I will." I set my mug down, feeling like a heathen for bringing it, and pulled up a chair. "So how have you been?" I buttered a croissant, my mouth watering in anticipation.

"Quite fine, dear," said Mom.

Mia poured a cup of tea into a ridiculously small teacup and handed it to me.

"Thank you." I added milk.

I took a bite out of my croissant. The freshly baked pastry tasted delicious. I gave a grateful nod to Mia and pointed to hers. "Eat, Mia."

She followed my lead, mirroring the way I buttered mine. The poor thing must have been starving. She rested her butter knife on the table and that look of disapproval from my mother made Mia place the knife back on her plate.

The tediousness of etiquette, I mused.

"What happened to your staff?" asked Mom.

"Gave them the day off."

She looked surprised. "You do that every weekend?"

"Pretty much, yes. How's the business?"

"Just wonderful," said Dad. "How's work?"

"Good and everything else too." I grinned over at Mia. "Quite perfect."

Dad arched a brow.

I took another sip of tea. "You moved your visit up?"

"Scheduling issues," he said. "Have a shareholder meeting tomorrow to discuss the advertising campaign." He went on to explain the specifics.

This was a man who ruled an empire with laser sharp perception and the fierceness of a successful CEO. He thought nothing of making the difficult decisions that had established Cole Tea as a leader in the beverage market. He was a visionary, taking one of the most traded agricultural commodities in the world and ensuring the Cole name remained one of the most popular brands.

We'd always been honest with each other, and now seemed like a good time to broach a sensitive subject. "Our latest commercial, Dad."

"What of it?"

"It's a little...shiny." I raised my hand in explanation. "Not sure it best reflects Cole Tea."

"I'm reassured by my team this current campaign perfectly reflects society."

"But do we want that?" I said. "Our branding has always been about sophistication. The client treating themselves to a luxury brand, and our price point—"

"Thought you had no interest in the business?" he said.

"You asked for my opinion on the commercial."

"Manhattan's Elite doesn't come cheap," he said. "They've made Bumble Soda a number one selling brand."

I forced a smile. "Whatever you think's best."

He looked defeated. "What can I tell you? I must trust my staff."

"Henry's looking forward to seeing you," I said.

Mom scoffed. "Not trying to get rid of us so soon?"

"We can invite him here."

"We're having dinner at the Ivy," said Dad.

"Mia and I are joining you." And on Mom's strained expression, I said, "We're not?"

"We want to discuss the business with him," said Dad. "You don't mind, do you?"

"Of course not," I said. "I imagine you have lots to talk about."

"And we know your thoughts on the subject," said Mom.

"I have other talents."

"He's an amazing doctor," said Mia.

Dad shifted toward me. "I'm glad he's out of Big Bear. Too much time to think."

"Cameron took him surfing yesterday," Mia said. "Henry had such a good time."

"Willow's through to the Pan American," said Mom.

"Show jumping," I told Mia. "My little sister loves horses." I reached for her hand and kissed her wrist.

Mia smiled coyly at my show of affection, blushing brightly.

"Aunt Rose sends her love." Mom jarringly changed the subject.

"Send our love to her," I said. "Rose is very fond of Mia."

"Son, when are you coming to see us?" She gave a knowing look. "We can invite the Taylors and their daughter, Maddie. You remember Maddie, don't you? She's at Stanford now."

"Mia, would you mind bringing us some more tea?" I said.

She pushed herself to her feet and lifted the tray with the silver urn.

In any other circumstance, I would have carried it for her. Mia walked away with the tray and I hated sensing their snobbery had hit its mark. I waited until she was out of earshot.

"Please be more respectful to Mia," I said firmly.

Mom gave a disapproving shake of her head and her lips pressed together, revealing there were words she knew not to say.

I didn't care for the superficiality of a world I'd never felt part of. Yes, I attended society events like the Dubai World Cup at the Meydon, or the Monaco Grand Prix, and loved attending polo matches, but for the sport, not to enter into a tedious conversation with a debutant looking to catch a husband. I didn't want that kind of woman.

My back stiffened. "Look, I care for Mia deeply. She's very special to me. And she's been through a dreadful ordeal. What she needs now is kindness."

"Ordeal?" said Dad.

"After Mia survived her mother's death, she came here to live with her father and his actions left her devastated. He betrayed her dreadfully."

Dad narrowed his gaze. "God, he didn't—"

"No, Dad," I snapped.

"How did her mother die?" asked Mom.

"Tragically," I said. "I have only one rule in this house, and that is we respect each other."

"You always did try to save wounded animals," she said. "Remember that dying bird you found in the garden? You tried to save it and your father had to sneak it off and snap its neck."

I feigned horror. "All this time I believed you'd sent that sparrow back to join the flock." Didn't share with them I'd watched my father do the deed. I'd been five at the time and clearly remembered it because one week later I'd been packed off to boarding school with a suitcase full of stiff uniforms, along with the kind of nightmares that followed me all the way to Harvard.

Mia wasn't that far away yet I missed her.

"I love her," I confessed.

"She's very pretty," said Dad. "A phase?"

I gave a look of annoyance.

"You're not really engaged?" asked Mom.

"You know the press," I said.

She flinched. "Press?"

"Tabloids," I clarified. "Don't worry Mom. Nothing's in Harper's Bazaar yet."

"Airtight prenup," said Dad.

"They're not getting married." Her high-pitch scraped my nerves. "Cameron just reassured us."

My headache was back.

"Altercation?" asked Dad.

I caressed my lip. "A misunderstanding."

"Please tell me it wasn't caught on camera."

"I don't believe so."

He gave that look of disappointment I knew so well.

"Here she is," said Mom, smiling convincingly at Mia.

The hairs on my nape prickled, fearing Mia might have overheard them.

"Would you like another croissant?" she asked. "I can make some more."

"We're fine," I said, rising to take the tray from her. "Thank you, Mia."

I waited until she sat and pushed her chair forward. I planted a kiss on her cheek and gave her shoulder an affectionate squeeze.

Returning to my seat, I led the conversation to my father's favorite subject, Cole Tea. Before long he'd relaxed again, and Mom even showed signs of enjoying him regale his latest business adventures. No doubt her brain was running through the subject of gene pools and breeding. An ideation close to her heart.

Dad reached down beneath the table and lifted a long cream colored scroll. Mom rose to clear the plates aside and Mia helped her.

These were the architectural schematics of a building. I leaned forward, my interest piqued by the elaborate design—a breathtaking crisscross of black glass showcased in a contemporary style. The vision of a sweeping skyscraper.

"Impressive, Dad. Where's this going?"

His eyes crinkled with excitement. "Here."

"Los Angeles?" I said.

Mia shot me a wary look.

"Construction is well underway," he said.

"It will create thousands of jobs," said Mom.

"The tallest building on the downtown skyline," added Dad.

My gaze rose to meet his and that familiar sense of doom came crashing back.

His fingertip trailed over the paper. "The view from the west will have fabulous sunsets."

I sat back, trying and failing to find the words to provide reason, to decline.

"You're looking at C. R. Cole Tower," he said proudly.

Mia took my hand and said wistfully, "Cameron, it's named after you."

CHAPTER 16

WELL THAT WAS pleasant.

It reminded me of the time I'd been plucked out of boarding school at age twelve one late summer afternoon and taken on a trip to South Africa by my parents. The visit became tainted when I strayed too far from the jeep and had the unsettling experience of being charged by a rhino. The animal's shortsightedness had saved the day.

With a forced grin and a wave goodbye, I watched my parents drive away in their chauffeured Bentley Continental. Mom seemed happy enough, and I'd managed to reassure Dad I'd give his offer serious consideration.

Stalling had become its own art form.

I locked the door and turned to rest my back against it, gathering what was left of my will to live.

A new vision promised to haunt my days. That architectural design was a threat in waiting. The building destined to tower above L.A.'s skyline would serve as a symbol of my Dad's disapproval.

I went in search of Mia.

Perhaps it was time to throw myself onto my sword and resign to the inevitable challenge of joining the family business. Resisting this centrifugal force pulling me apart felt futile and was doing crazy things to my head. My subconscious evoked the kind of nightmares that promised not to end unless I faced my fate. Every night, the same dream. Me, messing up one way or another, followed by an obvious wish fulfillment of needing to escape.

The level of interpretation that would make Freud proud: I'd lost a childhood to Cole Tea and was damned if I'd give that company my adult years as well.

I didn't want to think about that slow death now.

I needed *her*.

Needed to bask in her presence and breathe in her aura.

I knew my girl well.

Predictably, Mia was naked and swimming laps in the pool, cutting through the water with a determined pace. I glanced at the garden to make sure my parents hadn't left something behind and wouldn't return for it and catch my stunning Bohemian naked and strikingly rebellious.

Mia's love of water held an easy interpretation. This represented freedom to her, the ability to defy gravity and lose herself. If I ever saw a string of daisies in her hair, I wouldn't be surprised. There had to be hippy blood running through her veins.

I stood at the edge of the pool and called down to her. "They call it PTSD."

Mia swam toward me and peered up. "They just want the best for you."

"And what are you really thinking?" I said, amused.

"They don't like me, do they?"

Clenching my fists, I tried to suppress this building rage that my parents had hurt Mia. "They're old fashioned," I snapped. "Amongst other things."

"They don't approve of me," she said. "Do you think it was my tattoo?"

I knelt and reached out to run my fingers through her hair. "It's because you're wild, and beautiful, and untamable, and all that's wrong with this world is reflected in your profoundness."

Her eyes widened in wonder.

I rose to my feet and slipped off my tie, quickly unbuttoning my shirt. Undressed now, I dived in, swallowed up by the silence of the depth, swimming the full length until I reached her. Rising out of the water, I rested my back against the edge of the pool.

Mia tread water before me. "I'm sorry I let you down."

"How?"

"Maybe it was the croissants?"

I laughed. "Mia, you could have arranged a garden party and invited the Queen, and my mom would have found fault with it."

"What was it like growing up with that kind of scrutiny?"

"A perfect childhood," I said wryly. "Think Beatrix Potter on acid and you have a glimpse into the Cole nursery."

"You had a nanny?"

I bit my lip.

"Was she cruel to you?" she said softly.

"No, Bethany was a godsend. That was the problem. When my Mom realized how Henry and I had bonded with our nanny, Mom fired her."

"What happened?"

"We learned not to like our nanny's too much." He arched a brow. "Or at least not to show we did."

Her brow furrowed and I knew she was trying to connect that experience with how I was now.

"I wish I could have been there to save you," she said.

My heart flinched and I swallowed this wave of emotion as I reached out to her. "Boarding school saw to it no weakness was left in us."

Mia swam the short space and pressed her cheek against my chest. "Cameron."

I wrapped my arms around her, pulling her into me, closing my eyes and slipping into the sacredness of her. "Had I not tasted the bitterness of hell then how else could I truly appreciate what it is to spend time with you?"

She let out a deep sigh. "Not sure I can make up for all that."

"Trust me, you do."

I dipped my head and kissed her shoulder.

"I'm going to heal you," she whispered.

"You did, the moment you became mine." I cupped her face in my hands and kissed her firmly, passionately, tangling with her tongue for dominance and she let me in, let me lead her in our kiss.

Mia broke away and I held back on a moan of wanting her to remain in my arms.

She disappeared beneath the water, her mouth enveloping my cock, causing my body to jolt. A rush of excitement blazed through me. With her cheeks sucked in, she increased the pressure, sending a jolt of pleasure that stole my breath and had me gripping the edge, white knuckled.

Staring down at the blur of golden locks and bobbing head, the sensation taking me dangerously close, my concern for her was overshadowed by my dick's exultation of its nearing bliss. She used one hand to cup and massage my balls, while the other worked ingeniously with her mouth, up and down along the ridges of my erection.

A groan tore from me.

Her tongue now fully engaged in this symphony of talent. She wasn't the only one holding her breath. I couldn't breathe, couldn't talk, couldn't let go, my fingernails dug into stone, biceps twitching. This sensation of floating increased my arousal to fever pitch.

She was going to drown on my cock.

"Mia," I cried out.

Despite this primal defiance wanting her to see it through, I grabbed her arms and pulled her up and out of the water, both of us splashing, reaching out for balance.

Mia sucked in air, panting. A flash of mischief in her eyes was followed by laughter.

Her amusement was short lived. My need snatched all logic. Too engulfed in passion, I dragged her toward me and spun her round so her back lay against my front. I positioned my cock and thrust deep inside her, burying so far she cried out until I soothed her by playing with her sex in one hand and tweaking her nipples with the other. Her head lolled, her thighs shook, and her gasps revealed she'd surrendered completely.

"Mine," I whispered huskily.

"Yes."

Running my fingertip over her, flicking her clit just how she liked it, slow and firm, I mastered that small nub until it throbbed beneath my touch.

I remained still, waiting for her muscles to relax around my shaft. Her tautness gripped me, milking in time with the rhythm of my fingers.

The irony was not lost that my fear of my parents returning to see Mia sans clothes was now replaced by 'danger be damned.'

I was too far gone to care.

We ended up making love in the Jacuzzi.

And the shower.

And then back in the bed.

I'd soon be booking myself into sex rehab if this obsession continued. Our healthy sex life was morphing into a Shakespearean comedy. As though her sex exuded an elixir to life, and I needed it to survive. My carnal appetite was reaching new heights and I'd already earned myself the title of Lord of Chrysalis.

Just in case Mia needed time to decompress too, I gave her space to get dressed, *again*, for the day.

I headed down to the foyer and waited for her, taking the opportunity to call Shay back.

"Hey boss, what's up?" he said cheerily.

"Saw you have an update?"

"It's not good. We managed to get the number plate on the Kia—"

"The issue?"

"Came up stolen."

"And the face recognition match?"

"Baseball cap and glasses hid his face."

I caressed my brow. "So that's it?"

"Well, we're watching Mia, so if this guy reappears, we'll have him."

"Thanks, Shay. I appreciate the work you did on this."

"Anytime. Any plans for today?"

"My parents just visited. Now I'm off for some R & R with Mia."

"Will you please let us follow?'

"No, we'll be fine." I watched Mia heading down the staircase. She'd found the white summer dress and sunhat I'd laid out for her. She twirled on the stairs to show off her wide brimmed hat.

"Shay, take the day off," I said. "That's an order."

"Sure," he said. "You too."

"I intend to." I shoved my phone in my pocket. "Come here." I reached out for Mia's hand and pulled her into the alcove of the front door.

Reaching for the tube of sunblock resting on the hall table, I squirted some into my palm.

"Ms. Lauren," I said.

Mia assumed her pose: head down, eyes averted, and her hands held behind her back.

Taking my time, I applied cream to her face and she closed her eyes. That cute smile of happiness warmed my heart. I massaged the cream over her shoulders and upper back, and not wanting to stop there I eased off the straps of her dress and caressed sunblock over her breasts, rubbing it in and paying special attention to her nipples.

She swooned, jaw slackening, her body trembling.

I flicked up her straps. "Good girl. Now you're ready."

"Getting sunburned in winter," she said. "Only in Cali!"

"Couldn't live anywhere else."

"Maybe your dad knows that. Maybe that's why he's putting that building here."

"Let's not talk about it."

She wrapped her fingers around my hand and followed me out.

After assisting her inside the BMW, I climbed in and drove us out of the driveway and headed east.

"Where are we going?" she asked.

"Well, I thought I'd take my mermaid to her natural habitat."

She stared out the window. "Will Shay be there?"

I glanced over. "We're not going to Chrysalis."

"Where then?"

"You thought I was taking you to the water room?" I said, amused. "For further training?"

She gave an uncertain nod.

I smirked. "Maybe I will now."

"If it pleases you, sir."

"I just applied sunblock to your...well, my favorite assets."

"As if I missed that."

"Careful."

She perked up. "Where are we going then?"

"It's a surprise."

"Are we spending time alone?"

"Kind of."

"Now I am intrigued."

We drove the rest of the way with me holding her hand resting in her lap, listening to music, and enjoying the sunny drive to our destination.

Mia soothed my soul, and even though the day had started off shaky with my parent's unexpected visit, I was fast forgetting all that and savoring these moments. Mia would be the first woman I'd ever brought here. A sanctuary of sorts—a private escape that I only ever shared with Richard or Shay. A place where we could leave the world behind.

I turned off Admiralty Way onto Bali Way and parked in my reserved space. Hand in hand, Mia and I made our way up the boardwalk.

"Are we going on a boat?" she asked breathlessly.

"We are."

Her eyes widened as she took in the line upon line of yachts in every shape and size tethered to the dock. A vast collection of seafaring vessels, some designed for racing and others merely for the pleasure of cruising.

"Which one's yours?" she said.

"This one." I pointed to the small rowboat, its paint peeling, the blue tarp half in the water, an oar missing.

"It needs a lick of paint," she said.

"Wait a minute." I pulled her along the dock. "That's not my boat. Clearly it's been a while."

Mia laughed and hurried along beside me. Her face lit up when she saw the sleek yacht at the end. "Oh, look at that one."

"You like it?"

"It's amazing."

"Let's take this one then." I pulled her up the plank.

"Cameron!" She squeezed hand. "Is this yours?"

"Apparently."

It felt wonderful to be back on her. La Ricochet was my 57m Remington 5777 RIO luxury yacht and easily one of my more extravagant purchases from the last few years. Ricochet outshone the boats around her. I'd not been out on her in months.

Built with carbon glass and featuring the boldest lines, weighing 33OT, she was capable of a cruising speed of 29kts in the most challenging of ocean conditions. The supermodel of boats.

Keith Escobar appeared from the bow. "Hey there, Dr. Cole."

"Keith." I shook his hand firmly. "Good to see you. Thank you for being here."

"My pleasure. She's running well. That tweak to the engine worked wonders."

"Great to hear," I said. "May I introduce my girlfriend, Mia."

She took his hand and it was no surprise to see my sixty something weathered skipper completely taken with her.

With the introductions over, Keith headed back to the helm and Mia and I settled at the stern and huddled close as the boat eased away from the dock and we made a smooth transit out of the bay.

Marina Del Rey's harbor faded from view and the waterway opened up with houses and large stretches of land and condos lining the shore. With the climate warm and the breeze inviting, this really did feel like the perfect day.

We leaned on the balustrade and enjoyed the view, neither of us speaking, merely savoring our togetherness. This was one of the many traits I loved about Mia. She didn't fill the silence, drawing contentment with merely spending time with me and experiencing these new adventures.

"Warm enough?" I asked.

She brushed strands of hair out of her face. "Yes, you?"

I nodded and pulled her into a hug. "Once we get to Catalina Island, you can swim if you like."

"I need a swimsuit," she said, and on my smile added, "You really do think of everything, don't you?"

"Nothing gives me more pleasure, Mia, than seeing you happy."

"This is all so perfect."

I leaned against the railing and faced her. "You're the first woman I've brought on here."

"Cameron, you once told me…"

I lowered my gaze and read the sadness in her eyes. "Say it."

"You once told me that you only want what you can't have. Well you have me now?" She pressed her cheek over my heart.

"Listen, those words were spoken before I ever contemplated you'd become mine. Admit you are. That I own you. That'll you'll obey me in the bedroom. Surrender completely to all I do to you. That you understand your body is mine to fuck at will."

Her fingers scrunched my shirt. "Yes."

"Mia, there's something I have to tell you. I've wanted to since the first moment I met you, but I believed...well you know how it all went down. It became a mess because of me."

"Cameron."

"No, please, you must let me say this."

She gave a nod she would.

"You've been through so much because of the misjudged calls I've made. I've put you in danger, what with Lance and his desire for you and that debacle at Oberon Grove. Not to mention what I've put Richard through. I promise I'll always protect you. Be there for you. I marvel you're really mine. That you forgive my arrogance and respect my need to dominate."

She took my hand and kissed my palm.

"Mia, I fell for you that first day I saw you at Enthrall. But it was too late. Or so I thought. The plan was set. The game plan was underway and Richard needed you. I came to realize I need you too. But at that time, the best thing for everyone was to let you go. I came to understand the blinding truth." I stared off, hoping my words made sense. "When I'm not around you, the world feels wrong." I squeezed her hand. "Tell me I'm not scaring you."

"No."

"Our relationship is the most important part of my life."

"What about your family?"

"You and I couldn't be more right. They don't know me like you do."

She threw herself into my arms. "I'll always love you, Cameron. You save my life every day."

I dipped my head and kissed her. "Mia, love is just a word. That's all. I promise to show you how I feel by reminding you each day I don't take you for granted. I will honor you. Protect you. Shelter you from the storms before they even happen. I will worship you with my body, my mind, my heart, and my soul." I shook my head. "I'm fucking ridiculous. This, this is what you've done to me."

"I feel the same way."

"I promise to prove you've made the right decision."

She beamed up at me. "Guess what?"

"What?"

"We're going to sleep together tonight."

I let out a long sigh and hugged her to me.

We snuggled on one of the wicker couches and enjoyed the view from the deck, watching the world float by. This, our perfect escape.

We spent the rest of the day sunbathing, napping, and snuggling, and with the wind in our hair and the Ricochet's gentle rocking it felt like we'd found paradise.

We dined on lobster and shrimp salad, and no fun day out would be perfect without chocolate profiteroles. We fed them to each other, licking sauce off our fingertips, and savoring the taste of chilled champagne.

Afterward, Mia lay alongside me on the wicker lounger, resting her head on my chest, and I let out a long sigh of satisfaction.

"I want to ask you something important," I said.

She peered up at me. "Yes?"

"Would you be interested in taking over as director of my charities?"

She shifted to better look at me.

"I'm busy with work and Chrysalis, and I'm considering taking on a few more commitments with Cole Tea. I need someone I can trust. These organizations are close to my heart and I know you're the best person for the job."

"Cameron, I don't know what to say."

"Yes, would be nice."

Her face was flushed with excitement. "I would love to."

"Good." I hugged her into me. "That makes me happy."

"That's all I want."

"Then admit we'll always be honest with each other, kind, and quickly forgive each other's indiscretions."

"Indiscretions?"

"When we argue."

"Why would we argue?"

"Because we disagree?"

"I think we're too perfect to argue."

"Is this you trying to be funny?" I tickled her again.

Mia squirmed. "Well as you always like to be in charge, I doubt I'll have much say in the matter."

"Glad we clarified that."

"If I'm going to be running your charity I'm bound to have an opinion on things. So, you'll have to give me some lenience to make decisions on my own."

"I'm sure I can make allowances."

"Thank you for encouraging me."

I planted a kiss to her nose. "I want to see you fulfilled."

Her grin dazzled. "So sometimes I'll get to boss you around?"

I slid my hand beneath her bikini thong. "What do you think?"

Her jolt of pleasure revealed I'd hit the spot with my fingers.

"You were saying, Ms. Lauren?"

"We were discussing my obedience, sir," she breathed.

With my right hand, I grabbed a handful of golden locks and tugged her head back. "And your conclusion?" My fingertips flicked her faster.

Her wetness fired off my arousal.

"You are my master in all things."

"Good girl," I whispered into her ear. "And how do good girls get rewarded?"

She trembled against me, her face pressed against my chest, her groan of pleasure going on and on and on...

I plunged two fingers deep inside her, my thumb strumming her now, and she let out a deep throated cry as she climaxed—

Her endless moans were drowned out by the ocean.

CHAPTER 17

I'D CREATED A monster.

This sophisticated and exhaustively analytical psychotherapist who excelled with her patients by treating them with her certain brand of conciseness was now a royal pain in my ass.

Dr. Laura Raul, M.D. had come to work in my clinic right out of Yale, after a brief interview where Laura had wowed me with her comprehension of Jung's hypotheses, her ability to grasp complex theories, and her valedictorian status, along with her openness. All pointed to a healthy working relationship.

Right up until this moment.

Just yesterday I'd escaped to paradise on a yacht with Mia, and today I was back on dry land and regretting ever stepping off that boat.

"You've gone very quiet," said Laura.

"I'm thinking," I said. "Ruminating."

"Ruminating? About what?"

"Why I'm here."

It was the end of a long clinic day for us both and it wasn't unusual to take the occasional debriefing, but the mood was somehow different. Sitting opposite Laura, and uncomfortable that we were in her office and not mine, I too nursed a mug of coffee and mirrored the way Laura held hers, fully aware she knew it too.

It was out of character for her to flirtatiously hitch up her skirt like this, up above her knees to reveal her stocking tops. This hint of sensuality suggested a recent life change—the new affair kind. She'd kicked off her heels and tucked her legs beneath her. Her white shirt was crinkled, revealing she'd come from her new lover's house this morning and not her own Westwood Condo.

My thoughts returned to Mia, who'd spent the morning volunteering at Charlie's Soup Kitchen, and I couldn't wait to see her. Leo had texted me updates every half hour, per my request, and I didn't care how obsessed I looked.

Shay's men were also following her and I only hoped she hadn't realized. Still, Mia's potential annoyance was worth this peace of mind. The threat out there still lingered. And it darkened my heart that it always would.

Laura looked as equally distracted.

I'd left the door open to maintain an air of informality. Patricia, our secretary, wouldn't be able to overhear our conversation from her reception desk and, in here, Laura would know I didn't consider this a session.

I loosened my tie.

Laura kept her office an uncomfortable 73 degrees.

This sophomoric technique of overly heating the room, lulling the client and prying open their subconscious as though opening a clam, caused me to clench my jaw.

Yeah, no fucking way.

Giving a deep sigh of satisfaction, and playing along like this was all very cozy and I liked nothing more than talking about my personal life, I gestured for her to continue.

Laura smirked as though readying for the challenge to face off with me.

"We were talking about Mia?" she said.

"Nothing more to add," I said. "She's doing wonderfully." Of course I could have shared there had been a real breakthrough with unlocking Mia's darkest memory, and that she was now thriving as my lover, but this I chose to hold back.

Using BDSM to cure a patient had been a well-kept secret, right up until the board of psychiatry held a trial to inquire on its efficacy and predictably question its legality.

I'd dodged that bullet thanks to Mia's ingenuity. Her waywardness had its benefits, apparently.

"How did you do it, Cam?" said Laura. "How did you heal

Ms. Lauren?"

"I offered a safe and nurturing environment. One where Ms. Lauren felt comfortable to open up and talk."

Kept her locked up in a dungeon for days. That chain around her neck was a message to her subconscious that it had kept her tethered long enough. During her confinement I'd fed her, bathed her, and made love to her. Out of her sight, I'd analyzed the documents collated from her past. Mia had believed her entire life she'd shot herself up with cocaine and ridden the high while her mother lay dying of a drug overdose in the other room. I'd dissected the evidence gathered from Mia's home town and deciphered the clues, proving without a doubt she'd been injected by her mother's dealer.

A gentle easing of her recollection of that day, a delicate handling of the id, one of the three divisions of the psyche.

The verdict: Not guilty.

I'd freed the butterfly from the chrysalis and ensured her pathway to peace. The treatment had been radical, yes, but Mia was a changed woman because of it.

I let out a long sigh. "Mia responded well to traditional therapy."

Traditional, if your name was Carl Jung.

Laura went to speak.

"Who is he, Laura?" I said.

"Who?"

"Your latest conquest."

"It's a little complicated."

"Isn't it always?"

She took a sip. "Why does it have to be that way?"

I took a sip. "Why does it have to be that way?"

"I expect more from the great Dr. Cole."

I grinned. "Apparently the sex is great."

She rolled her eyes. "How do you do that?"

"How do I do it, Laura?"

She narrowed her gaze. "My desire to talk about myself, my need for your validation, my post climatic blush."

"I see everything."

She pursed her lips seductively. "And I see everything too, Cam."

No, she did not.

"Ah, well there you have me, Laura." I took another sip.

"McKenzie," she said.

"What about her?"

"We've had several sessions. She's been very forthcoming about your relationship."

"I'm not comfortable with where this is going," I said. "We're heading into personal territory."

She gestured to her desk. "I'm comfortable with you reviewing McKenzie's file. I'd appreciate your opinion."

"I'm not sitting in a session with her, Laura."

"Hear me out."

I gestured I'd listen at least.

"You both experienced a trauma. You both need to heal. This is a great opportunity for you, Cameron, to…"

Don't fucking say it.

Laura fidgeted. "I know you hate the term closure, but McKenzie has questions and you have the answers."

"What does she want to know?" I said flatly.

"Face to face, Cameron."

"I don't see what good it will do."

"I have determined this is what's best for my client. You and I both utilize unusual techniques." She lowered her gaze. "You more than me. Trust me on this, I know what my patient needs and I'm asking you—"

"Laura—"

She raised her hand to cut me off. "Let me finish, please. My client is undergoing infertility treatment. She has residual post stress that needs resolution if her treatment stands any chance of success."

"You can't pin her inability to conceive on me—"

"Perhaps at a subconscious level?"

With a shake of my head, I refused to accept such a warped view. "I didn't see a ring."

"You saw her?" she said. "When?"

"Evidently you haven't spoken with Zie since New Year?" I said. "I bumped into her at a party. We chatted. Briefly. Not long enough for her to tell me she was married or in a relationship." I shrugged. "She didn't want children when we were together."

"I've taken the privilege of arranging a session."

"When?"

"How does in half an hour sound?"

Like hell.

"You went ahead and booked this without speaking with me first?" I seethed. "Perhaps I have an appointment—"

"I know you well, Cameron. I know your routine."

"Really?"

"Why, yes. You run two or three miles every morning," she said.

Make that six to ten, depending.

"You attend clinic in the morning," she said. "Then afterwards you visit your private men's club."

Chrysalis. The place Laura didn't know existed.

She gave a nod of confirmation. "While at the club, you play a round of tennis and share drinks with your friends."

More accurately, while at Chrysalis I check in with the doms and their subs and then visit the stables, where young men with pony fetishes role play with tails inserted in their asses and hour long erections. Men who'd be otherwise condemned by society, and the only way they function at an optimum level in life is to fulfill their penchant in a safe and nurturing environment, with Dominic as their stable master.

Laura pulled her legs out from under her and sat squarely facing me. "And then you go home to that big house of yours and have wild, unadulterated sex with some young woman you've seduced. A woman who probably won't hear from you again after you've turned her life upside down."

Before Mia, I'd wandered my Beverly Hills mansion alone, the only respite those cherished fencing sessions with Shay. Or delving into my beloved books in my library in an effort to hold back the loneliness.

"God you're good, Laura."

"Cam, I need you to respect my judgment call on this one, okay?"

Fuck.

"We'll get this out of the way and you can both move on. She can move on."

I glanced at my watch. Mia would be here soon and I hated the idea she might bump into Zie.

"Push your plans, Cameron," she said. "We only need an hour. Then it's over."

"And Zie will leave me alone?"

"Yes, I believe this will go a long way to making that happen."

I relented with a nod.

"Well done," she said.

Tugging on my shirt cuffs one at a time, I ran through all the ways I could have handled this better, like questioning Laura on why she'd refurnished her office in this European flair, or where she'd purchased that print by Lilly Drey, the artist having a knack for capturing the curves of voluptuous women.

This wasn't Laura's style.

And I'd not seen her wear that shade of lipstick before.

"How long have you been seeing this guy?" I asked.

She waved it off. "Oh, and if you feel the need for Mia to have any more sessions with a therapist, my door's always open. As Mia's fiancé, you can't treat her. As you well know."

"We're not engaged," I said. "A misunderstanding. I've clarified our position with my family. We'll make a public announcement once everything has settled down."

"Settled down?"

"The psychiatric board's trial is behind us. Yes, the case is closed, but there's formalities. Legal fine tuning."

"I'm curious," she said. "How would you define your relationship with Mia?"

"Private."

"Do you ever see yourself marrying her?"

"Mia's remarkable."

"You didn't answer my question, Cam."

"She's a breath of fresh air."

"Perhaps it would be unwise to leave another woman decimated in your wake," she said flatly, slicing through my dignity with the shrewdness of a well-practiced bitch.

I had the perspicuous skills to perform the fencing equivalent of an Attaque au Fer and take Laura so far down the path of self-hate she'd not recover.

I felt merciful and offered a polite smile.

"You once told me McKenzie was the closest you'd ever come to getting hitched." She lowered her gaze. "Zie is very compelling."

"Yes, she is."

"A brilliant mind and body to die for," she said. "Most men wouldn't have let her go so easily."

"And your point?"

"You loved her so much you didn't believe you were worthy of such an incredible woman."

"Oh, I'm worthy."

Laura looked offended.

"Ever consider I'm protecting Zie from you?" I said. "After all, we spent a great deal of time together and we shared a rare intimacy." I broke Laura's gaze as a memory flashed into focus.

Regret swept over me like a dark cloud of guilt. I'd not handled Zie's predilections well. I should've pulled her back from the brink before she'd indulged her darkest desires. Zie's insatiable need to push herself into the very center of debauchery fractured everything we'd built. She'd turned something beautiful, *us*, into a sordid mess, leaving me with nothing but the memory of never being enough.

"Any change of heart in your future?" asked Laura.

"With Zie?" I resisted scoffing.

Laura shifted uncomfortably. A small blush colored her cheeks.

I ran through my words to see what had rattled Laura. My gaze settled on her trash can beneath her desk and I ruminated on why my subconscious was leading me to look at it.

The phone rang in my office.

"We were talking about marriage?" said Laura.

"Love can't be defined by a legal document—"

"We humans are so infallible," she said.

My iPhone buzzed and I glanced at a text from Shay: *Fencing still on?*

Shay couldn't go more than five days without challenging me. And challenge me he did. His deftness with a blade was unsurpassed. Agreeing to another match was my way of maintaining his pride because I ruled him in every other way.

Seven I texted back.

"Everything okay, Cameron?"

I tucked my phone back into my pocket. "Yes."

"We were discussing how contracts are inevitably breeched," Laura said.

"And who wants to keep a vow that states for better or for worse?" I said. "Who settles for fucking worse?"

Mia stood in the doorway.

She raised the paper bag she was holding. "I brought you a pastry from Charlie's," she said meekly. "And one for you too, Dr. Laura."

"That's very sweet of you, Mia," said Laura, hiding her cringe.

Mia's uncertain gaze found me again.

CHAPTER 18

MIA'S FINGERS SCRUNCHED the paper bag.

Other than that, her face returned to calm.

I rose to my feet and said, "Mia, let's go to my office."

With a quick nod to Laura to let her know she'd done enough damage for today, I took Mia's hand in mine and led her into my office.

I shut the door and locked it.

Mia placed the paper bag on my desk and gracefully strolled over to the window. The way her blue eyes caught mine reflected forgiveness even in the wake of cruelty. Yes, she was strong, but vulnerable too, and this made me feel like I'd captured a rare creature.

And just hurt her.

"Mia," I whispered.

Her silhouette caught the morning light streaming in and sunshine shimmered off wisps of her golden locks. She appeared ethereal. Her petite frame hid the fact she could be feisty, and the passion burning within her would floor any man. She was so damn beautiful and each time I saw her again I was stunned by how dazzling she was.

I pinched the bridge of my nose. "Mia, you heard part of a conversation—"

She spun round. "I'm only twenty-one. Who says I want to get married yet anyway?"

A wave of concern hit me when I realized she wasn't wearing her collar.

"Mia, let me explain—"

"It's fine."

"It's not fine." I moved toward her. "What you heard was out of context."

She cupped my face with her hands. "If all I had was today to love you, it would be more than most women have in a lifetime. You've given me so much, Cameron. Shown me so much. I don't regret one second of it, and if you and I ever became more it wouldn't be something I'd take for granted. It would be a miracle that we found each other and that we're so perfect for each other."

She melted against my chest and I hugged her, closing my eyes, drawn into this moment, soothed by her gentleness. I breathed in her delicate perfume.

A spellbinding scent that both comforted and fired my senses.

Pure Mia.

"Are you doing okay?" she whispered, her expression full of concern.

I relented with a nod. "Laura pushed a few buttons and I failed to subdue my response."

"You sit there and I'll sit here." She sat in my therapist's chair, gesturing to the large black wooden carved leather seat opposite. The chair reserved for clients.

I folded my arms and stared at her.

"We'll talk," she said. "You can tell me what's upset you. Go on, sit."

"Up." I grabbed her hand. "Sit here."

We made our way over to the large sofa and she kicked off her shoes.

I sat beside her. "Where's your collar?"

Her fingers traced her throat. "Didn't want to wear it to Charlie's," she said. "Didn't seem right."

Brushing a stray hair out of her face, I marveled at her thoughtfulness. Her gaze was kind and understanding—blue irises overshadowed by revealing dilated pupils.

A stab of doubt.

I always saw too much.

"What buttons did Dr. Laura push?" she asked.

I began cautiously. "Laura believes it will be good for McKenzie if we have a session together."

"You and McKenzie?"

"Laura will be present."

Mia looked thoughtful. "Sounds a little awkward."

"Yes, well there were two options on the table. This or the other one, which is to gouge my eyes out with a burning hot spoon. Right now it's the front runner."

She smiled. "Why?"

"Zie feels ready to face her demons and apparently I'm one of them." I shrugged. "Laura has assessed her case and believes this will provide closure for her client."

"Thought you didn't believe in closure?"

"No, but I do believe in at least finding some solution to pain. There's guilt on my part. And Zie needs to be handled."

"You have my support. Whatever you believe is best."

I took her hand in mine. "Mia, I want you to know there's no residual feelings for Zie." She went to speak and I rested my fingertips on her lips. "I love you, and what is testament to how wonderful we are is us sitting here and talking calmly."

"Yes, I do love how easy you are to talk to." She rummaged in her handbag. "And I suppose now's a good a time as any. I made a few amendments." She handed me the folded up piece of paper.

I unraveled it and stared down at the non-disclosure agreement Dominic had emailed to Mia.

This very document had been provided to all previous girlfriends and contained the legalese ensuring that should we ever end our relationship, my personal life would remain so and not find its way in a tabloid or worse still on some TV expose. The settlement provided after the dissolution of a relationship was overly generous, or so Dominic had told me. A formality I didn't deal with.

Mia had scribbled on the form.

"I don't want your money." She pointed. "I signed it, scanned it, and emailed it back to Dominic. He told me I have to talk to you about the pay off."

"Pay out, Mia, not payoff. It's to compensate you."

"I don't want your money, Cameron. I've told you that. In fact that was the other thing I wanted to talk to you about."

I raised my gaze to meet hers. "Go on."

"I want to keep working at Enthrall."

I sat back, feeling as though the air had been sucked out of me. With her out of my sight, I couldn't watch over her. She'd be vulnerable.

"With Richard as your boss?" I said.

"Of course."

"Out of the question."

"Well I can't work at Chrysalis," she said. "I can't date my boss again. It put everyone in an awkward position."

Yes, well there were mitigating circumstances, including and not limited to using Mia to trap my best friend into a relationship. Richard could ignore the girls at the high-end bars but he'd have been hard pushed to ignore the innocent attending to his every need as his secretary. And those FMB's Mia had unwittingly worn provided a splash of genius.

Jealousy swept over me that Richard had ever touched her.

"As the director, I decide on which employees work where." I rose and moved over to my desk. "I profile and ascertain who is the best fit and where."

Mia realized I was serious. She pushed to her feet. "I need to make a living, Cameron."

I shook the mouse to awaken my computer and searched my files.

"You were just saying how wonderful it is we can talk?" She moved over to me. "I need to be independent."

"No, you think that, but in reality life will be much easier for you if you let me take care of everything."

"Are you saying I can't work?"

I caressed my brow. "We had this conversation, remember? In London."

Confusion marred her face.

I turned toward her. "I warned you that should you become mine the experience would be one of intense ownership. That I would possess you beyond all understanding."

Mia gazed up at me.

"I distinctly recall telling you I'd overpower every aspect of your life. Completely dominate you, and while I was at it I'd most likely fuck you half to death." I smirked.

Her eyelids fluttered as she teetered toward subspace.

She broke from it and whispered, "What about what I want?"

"Mia, you are not my prisoner." I gestured to the door. "I won't prevent you from doing what makes you happy."

"Unless it's where I work."

"For now, yes."

I wanted to tell her I had to keep her safe and my possessiveness was about protecting her. Not wanting to scare Mia, I turned away and opened a file. I needed the distraction for this conversation to end.

"Don't go cold on me," she said.

"I'm not, sweetheart." I pulled her into my chest and hugged her.

"I feel safe with you." She wrapped her arms around my waist. "I don't want to leave you."

"You're been transferred over to Chrysalis," I said. "You're my executive assistant now."

Mia's demeanor shifted and she stepped back. "What about Enthrall?"

I lifted the receiver and speed dialed Richard's office.

"Booth," answered Richard sharply.

"Hey," I said. "How are you?"

"Missing a secretary."

"That's why I'm calling."

Silence.

"Scarlet's on it," I said. "Any requests?"

"This is my sandbox. Find your own toy. Oh wait, you did. Mine."

"I have tickets for the Lakers."

"Always did like you."

"Good. Please inform Ms. Lauren of her transfer."

He scoffed. "How's your day going? Interestingly annoying as well by the sound of things?"

"How are you?"

"Why'd you call me?"

"I'm handing the phone over to Ms. Lauren."

Mia took the phone. "Hello, Richard. We were just discussing me coming back to Enthrall."

Her frown deepened as she listened. "Can we talk about it?"

Her eyes darted to mine.

I circled my finger for her to hurry it up.

She handed the phone back.

The line was dead. Richard had hung up.

"Well?" I said.

"He fired me."

"Glad we got that squared away."

She rested her hands on her hips. "What will my duties be?"

"Your secretarial duties will continue. As will your training. Also, your lessons. Your future is my priority."

She swallowed her nervousness. "Will I be allowed to wear clothes?"

That visual threw me off.

No, was a tempting answer.

The hum of the printer called my attention. I picked up the fresh version of the non-disclosure Mia had amended and handed it to her. "If you ever tamper with any legal document of mine in the future, there will be consequences, Ms. Lauren."

She stared down at the fresh agreement. "But I don't like it."

"Irrelevant. This—" I pointed to it—"ensures your financial security, should things not work out between us."

"You don't think things will work out?"

"Mia, this is business. Sign it and let's forget about it."

She held it up. "Don't you think we're telling the universe we're not going to make it?"

"It also protects me should you ever decide to sell your story—"

"Not after everything you've done for me."

I caressed my brow. "Mia, perhaps talk with Dominic about this? He handles the legalese."

She moved over toward the shredder and turned it on. "I'm not a business dealing."

I narrowed my gaze. "Don't even think about it."

The shredder ate the form.

I glared at her. "That was your first mistake, Ms. Lauren."

She drew her teeth over her bottom lip and sucked it.

That really wasn't helping.

A step closer. "Perhaps you might be interested to know your second mistake?"

Her subtle nod.

"You have forgotten who I am," I said darkly.

She neared me and her eyes widened, her lips slightly parted.

I reached out and tipped her chin up. "I will not be defied. By anyone."

"Yes, sir," she breathed.

"This world has the potential to destroy your soul. I will not stand by and allow anyone to hurt you. Ever. I will always watch over you."

Mia twisted her mouth thoughtfully.

"Usually Dominic deals with these details, but I can see you need persuading. Let's go over this—" with a click of the mouse, I printed off another form —"line by line until you understand its importance."

"I won't sign anything that mentions you giving me money," she said. "So delete that bit and I'll sign it right now."

"Mia, it gives me peace of mind to know you'll be taken care of."

"I love you for you."

"Mia, please—"

"Perhaps I'll go and work for Cole Tea," she said. "Maybe Henry wasn't joking about the job offer."

"The job's based in San Francisco."

"I don't want to leave you."

I held back on a laugh. "Then don't."

"Are you angry?"

"I am considering which discipline best suits your defiance."

Her face flushed brightly.

"As soon as I get you home," I said. "There will be no lenience in your punishment."

Mia dropped to her knees and looked up at me. "Sir." She reached for my zipper and pulled me out of my pants. "You understand why I say these things, because"— she licked the full length of my shaft from balls to tip —"I care about you, about making you happy."

Eyes closed, I felt her tongue urging my persuasion. Her lips wrapped tight around the head and sucked pre-cum from me. That sensual sound of her suckling…

A knock at the door startled us.

"Dr. Cole?" came Patricia's voice. "Your five-thirty is here."

Otherwise known as an invitation to purgatory.

"I'll be right there," I called out to her.

"I'll let Dr. Laura know, sir," she said and walked away.

I peered down at Mia. "Continue."

Obediently, she took me all the way to the back of her throat and I savored this moment, delaying the inevitable torture waiting in the other room.

My gaze drifted to the wall and lingered on Caravaggio's 1571 print *The Conversion on the way to Damascus*, the depiction of Paul on his way to persecute Christians in Damascus, though now the subject lay flat on his back, having fallen off his horse after being struck by light and blinded by God. Paul's stunned expression was overshadowed by his horse, the animal merely a shadow above him.

Paul lay helpless.

Caravaggio's genius was in the way he communicated his subject's feelings, that we were able to experience their horror when we viewed the painting.

It was time to wedge shut the door to the past, and I was even prepared to psychologically nuke the situation if needed.

"Up." I stepped back from Mia and tucked myself away.

She rose to her feet and blinked, as though not sure if she'd pleased me.

Affectionately, I stroked her flushed cheek. "Wait here."

"Yes, sir."

I walked over to my satchel and pulled out my laptop. "Access my Chrysalis emails. Answer as many as you can."

"Yes, sir."

I needed to keep her occupied.

Setting the laptop down on my desk, I said, "The code to get in is your name."

Her fingers traced over her lips. Her eyelids were still heavy.

I hated leaving her.

"And while you wait, consider this fact, Ms. Lauren."

"Sir?"

"If you don't sign that form by the time I return, you'll never experience my cock again."

I left her to think about it.

CHAPTER 19

ONE THOUGHT OF McKenzie and goodbye erection.

After a knock on Laura's office door, I was invited in.

Back straight and on guard, I felt ready to face off with whatever Laura had in mind, as well as having to sit in the same room as Zie.

The two women rose to greet me. A waft of Hermes. The scent of sex and war.

What does any good man want? Love, of course. We're not so different. We fall just as deeply. Afterward, when the fairytale is over and all affection has dissipated and the relationship lost its shine, love's spark snuffed by cruel words spoken, the desecration of what was once sacred, the no going back monologues spoken with bitterness, endless screamed rants of pain and betrayal leave us lesser men.

We too have to claw our way back.

The woman who'd once been my everything stood before me in a blur of powder blue Chanel, curls of auburn locks, and pale pink lipstick highlighting her heavily outlined eyes. A stunning vision of sensuality.

Even Laura's gaze lingered on her client, as though awed by Zie's beauty and just as taken by her commanding aura. I'd endured that sting of Zie's Scorpio tail too many times to find any pleasure in being here.

Zie stepped forward, nudging my hand away when I offered it.

"Silly, there's no formality between us." She hugged me tight, pressing her yoga fit body against mine.

"You look well, Zie." I pulled out of her hold and moved over to the seat opposite theirs.

"Again I want to reiterate, Dr. Cole," said Laura as she sat back down. "How much we appreciate you taking the time to explore some issues McKenzie is having. Perhaps with us all on the same page we'll find a resolution for her."

"Glad to help in any way I can," I said.

Mia was on the other side of that wall and it surprised me how much comfort that gave. I hoped she'd signed that form, seen reason. She deserved every cent from having been my lover, should we not work out. I leaned forward to ease the stab to my heart that thought gave me.

Laura rested her iPad on her lap, ready to take notes. "I respect this isn't easy for you."

"Must we?" I gestured to the iPad.

"Yes."

"Thank you for doing this," said Zie, holding a smile I didn't recognize on her.

Laura continued to coax Zie from her previous visit, building on her therapeutic alliance and setting the frame of the session. As a fan of Freud, Laura's questioning assisted Zie to explore her subconscious through free association in an endeavor to reveal the connections that might have lain hidden.

Laura's unmasking of Zie's subconscious went as expected.

"Perhaps I do see my father in Cameron," said Zie. "Dad's strong, influential, and cold at times. Unobtainable. Did you know he's on his third wife?"

"No, I didn't," I said.

"Perhaps, Cameron, you're right about a father complex," said Laura softly. "Let's examine this further, Zie?"

Zie crossed a long, lean leg over another, showing off her well-toned calves and closing down this line of discussion. "I've been replaced by a younger woman. How predictable."

"Are you referring to Cameron's latest girlfriend?" said Laura.

"I haven't seen you in years," I countered.

Zie's gaze drifted toward my office wall. "Is she still here?"

"She is."

145

"Is Mia in therapy too?" Zie threw her head back in a laugh. "Jeez, Cameron, all your women are fucked up."

"This is about us Zie, about our past," I said. "What we once had."

"Dr. Cole, your current girlfriend may reflect your state of mind," said Laura.

"If you're referring to my constant state of happiness," I said, "you might be onto something there, Laura."

She gave a disapproving glare.

"We were happy." Zie sounded vulnerable. "Once."

I regretted my outburst. "How's work?"

"Very good. I have a gallery showing in New York in a month. Perhaps you'd like to come?"

Her double entendre was lost on Laura.

The games had begun.

There was a strong desire to question Zie on her new relationship, on her infertility treatment, a need to know what she'd done with the years since I'd seen her, but I knew it was better to let Laura continue to lead the session.

"McKenzie," said Laura. "You wanted to ask Cameron about Willow?"

The hairs prickled on my nape.

"Did you tell your sister to block my calls?"

I shifted in my seat. "Apparently the last time you met with my sister your conversation featured me?"

"She told you that?"

"Yes."

"I merely wanted to make sure you're making good decisions."

"That was kind of you," I tried to sound convinced. "Did Willow manage to reassure you?"

"She mentioned Mia's a free spirit," said Zie. "Willow didn't go into detail, but from the gist I was surprised you'd settled for such an inexperienced girl."

I glanced over at Laura. "I was under the impression we were here to talk about Zie?"

"You prefer a submissive personality," said Zie.

A strike to my bow. Zie knew my BDSM lifestyle was guarded fiercely.

"Irrelevant," I said.

"I'm more likely to stand up for myself," said Zie. "Not be bullied."

"I don't bully, and Mia's perfectly capable of standing up to me," I said. "Trust me, it's one of the many traits I admire in her."

Zie sat up straight. "You once told me the only way a relationship has any chance of surviving is if both set of parents approve."

"That does factor in, yes."

"Both of our parents approved of us Cameron. They've remained good friends."

"So I hear."

"Your parents haven't met Mia's?"

"Mia's mother died when she was a teenager."

"And her father?"

"There's still time," I said, refusing to reveal there'd be no introduction of Mia's Dad to my parents—a fact that still unsettled me. "Zie, where are you going with this?"

"I still care deeply for you," she said. "There is," — She glanced over at Laura – "I have faith you'll come round to see I'm the right woman for you."

Laura had visibly paled. Her fingers clenched around her iPad, as though mulling over how to deflect this conversation.

"Laura informed me you're undergoing infertility treatment?" I deflected for her.

"Yes. Perhaps a baby…"

"Born out of love with parents in a healthy relationship, if you want my advice."

"Perhaps you might consider donating?" said Zie.

"Donating?"

"Your sperm."

I scratched my jaw, wondering if Richard might find this conversation just as startling later when I recounted it. Yes, it would be considered breeching confidentially, but I needed to be talked back off the ledge of insanity.

"Your current partner is infertile?" I asked gently.

"I'm dating a woman."

"I see."

"Perhaps if we explore why you didn't work out?" Laura said.

"Cameron, would you share with McKenzie why those final days ended the way they did?"

I shot a look at Zie.

"You told me you would always love me," she said.

"Those were hard days for me too."

"Do you still love me?"

Laura sat forward and rested her hand on Zie's knee. "You don't stop loving someone just because you're no longer together, Zie."

This was totally out of line.

Laura was off her game, and I wondered if her current relationship was warping her perspective and skewering her analysis.

"Cameron?" Zie said.

"I care for you deeply. That's why I'm here. I want you to move on. Have the life you want."

"Mia isn't right for you. Your parents disapprove."

"And how would you know that?"

"Because I know your mom, Cameron. She'll hate the idea of you marrying Mia with her background. She's not one of us."

I glanced at the wall clock. The hands hadn't moved since the last time I checked.

"Loyalty is important to you," she said. "You don't tolerate infidelity."

"Zie." I stared into her eyes, wondering if she was prepared to take this all the way to truth.

"We had the kind of relationship that allowed for exploration," she said.

"Yes, but you took it too far."

"Cameron, you run the manor."

A threat to blow my private life wide open.

My glare left Zie and slid over to Laura. "Would you mind stepping out a moment?"

"It's best I stay."

My gaze returned to Zie, daring her to go there and reveal the existence of Chrysalis, share with Laura the intimate details of nights spent exploring the most decadent scenes, and even further into the darkest abyss of the psyche. The rawest memory of why we'd not made it.

Remaining focused and wary, I tried to pull this conversation back. "Zie, there are extraordinary private issues that we share. Perhaps if we talk in a private setting?"

"Laura knows."

My gaze shot to Laura "Knows what exactly?"

"About the Harrington Suite," said Zie. "And what we did in it."

"What you did in it," I corrected.

"I was young and easily influenced."

"No, Zie, you fully consented. You wanted to be in there. Chose to be there. If you recall correctly, I wasn't meant to be there that night."

That night. When I'd left work at 1AM with a 102.0 fever and had another doctor take my shift, stopping off at Chrysalis to find my lover in the Harrington Suite. Zie, the director's woman, had been the center of attention and immersed in the kind of vision reserved for hardcore films.

Standing in the shadows of that ballroom, I'd watched my fiancé being taken by man after man in an endless orgy. A continuous fucking that had no end in sight. My thoughts spiraled, trying to grasp this surreal vision within what had felt like a fever-dream.

The days that followed had me nursing myself back from both the flu and the heartbreak of realizing we were over.

Zie had not only betrayed me but turned my house into a perversion, ruining all I held dear. This carefully managed sanctuary, this home I'd created for those who lingered on the edge of society, had morphed into an iniquitous mess.

"Are you going to pervert Mia, too," asked Zie.

"You're a nymphomaniac," I said softly. "Mia is not."

"Perhaps if we refrain from labeling," said Laura.

"Well, as her actions in the Harrington Suite are up for discussion," I said, "what are your thoughts on the issue, Laura?"

"I'm not here to judge, Cameron. Merely explore and find resolution for you both."

I shrugged. "I've moved on. What can I do, Zie, to convince you as well?"

"You fuck Mia every day," said Zie. "Countless times, if your appetite is the same as it was with me."

"And your point?"

"You're not enough for her."

I shook my head, annoyed with how she'd derailed this session.

"Mia and I are just fine."

"We were fine, Cameron. You and Mia have cracks in your relationship."

"And how would you know that?"

Zie's gaze left mine and she held Laura's stare.

Anger welled with her insinuation.

"All sessions are confidential," said Laura.

My jaw tightened. "If there has been any discussion of my private life—"

"I get you, Cameron," said Zie. "I'm the only woman who can fulfill you. Satisfy your predilections."

"McKenzie," said Laura. "You told me you were happy in your relationship now and it gave you the stability you need?"

Zie's glare stayed on me. "You're going to get hurt, Cam."

"What gives you that idea?"

Her eyes sparkled. "Mia's having an affair."

"What are you talking about?"

"You have no idea, do you?"

Laura's iPad was face down on her lap, her gaze jumping from me and back to Zie, her obvious loss of control overruled by her intrigue.

"Mia's always been close to Richard," I said.

"Not Richard," she said. "Though they were fucking once, weren't they, before you stole her?"

"It wasn't like that."

"Mia has a special friend at Charlie's. I imagine you thought her enthusiasm to work there was down to her charitable nature."

"You're wrong."

"He's one of the other volunteers." She looked triumphant. "They're quite the couple, apparently. Sneaking off to talk privately. Mia's a bundle of nerves when he's around. Like a schoolgirl."

"You're lying."

"I still have friends from when I worked there."

"One shift—"

Was all she'd fucking managed.

"Rebecca told you this?" I said.

"Yes."

Rebecca, the woman I'd entrusted to run my soup kitchen based on the fact she'd been the best candidate to take my charity café where it needed to go. She was to feed the homeless and provide a safe refuge when they ate their only meal of the day. And not take any bullshit. Apparently Rebecca also had a thing for gossip and had no taste in friends.

"What did Rebecca tell you exactly?" I said.

"All I know is that it's the only time you're not on Mia like a rash," said Zie.

"Got a name?"

"Nope. Apparently he's cute though. Tattooed and very hot. All the girls at Charlie's swoon over him. Rides a Harley. He's young. More Mia's age."

"Good luck with everything, Zie." I pushed myself to my feet, hoping I'd make it to the door without punching the wall.

"We're not done here," said Laura.

I strolled back toward her, picked up her iPad, and with several swipes on the screen I deleted all record of our session.

"Hey," said Laura. "You can't do that."

I handed it back to her. "Just did."

Taking a deep breath of reason, I headed for the door.

I'd just been exposed to lunacy in its purist form.

CHAPTER 20

LINCOLN PICKED UP on this awkward silence.

Swapping wary glances with me, his usual humor suppressed, he kept his gaze averted as he served us dinner.

The silence was palpable.

Mia sat opposite me on the other side of the long dining room table. She hadn't touched her food and neither had I. We merely sipped mineral water, lost in our own thoughts. Other than the dim light shining down from the chandelier above, the room was pretty dark. I liked it this way. It matched my mood.

Lincoln had been in my service for years. He'd lost his house after he'd been fired from his job as a server at Zona's Café, after snapping back at the young manager over some trifle issue.

He'd volunteered at Charlie's in an attempt to get his life back on track. I'd hired him soon after and provided a generous employment package when he came on as my butler.

Lincoln knew well enough not to engage me in conversation when I was this quiet. He merely placed our food before us and headed out.

Mia watched Lincoln close the door behind him. "He's nice."

"Ex-convict," I said.

Her gaze snapped up.

I smirked. "Pot possession."

"Was he a dealer?"

"No, he broke his back in a car accident and was using it for pain relief, back when it was illegal."

"And you know this for sure?"

I narrowed my gaze. "Being able to read when people are lying comes in handy."

Her fingers traced over her throat.

She'd dressed for dinner in the black halter-neck dress I picked out. Her hair was down, just as I liked it, and her makeup natural. She looked ethereal under this yellow light.

"How long has Lincoln worked for you?"

"Five years."

She gave a nod, as though mulling that over. "Cameron, you didn't ask me."

I took a sip of water.

"About the contract," she spoke softly.

"What about it?"

"I thought you might ask if I signed it."

I unraveled my napkin. "I find this subject boring."

"Was it difficult seeing her again?"

"It went as expected."

"How?"

I shrugged.

"Cameron?"

"She was always a bitch, but she's something altogether different now."

"Why did you date her if she was like that?"

I arched a brow. "Mia, there'll be no dissecting my past relationships for your listening pleasure."

"I didn't mean—"

"Yes, you did."

"Was she cruel to you?"

"She pushes my buttons." I gave Mia a *so do you* look.

She nudged her plate away. "She wants you back?"

"She's in a relationship."

My mind drifted to our session and I tried to tie together the evidence of what had been said, as well as what had gone unsaid, all of it providing clues to why Zie wasn't satisfied in her new relationship. If only I could focus my thoughts I'd be able to unravel these dark secrets and the truth would spill.

"The way she looked at you—"

"Eat." I gestured to her plate. "Considering you spent the day feeding the hungry, don't you think it's inappropriate to take a good meal for granted?"

"Maybe we should sell that." She pointed to the chandelier. "Give the money to Charlie's."

"Sure, if you like sitting in the dark."

We'd turned the corner of irrationality.

Her gaze slid over her entree.

Steak, rare, bloody. Asparagus soaked in a bright red juice.

"Something wrong, Mia?" I said coldly.

"I ordered the salmon."

"We can't always have what we want."

Her brow furrowed. "It was on the menu."

"So tell me how your day was? How are the staff at Charlie's?"

She held my gaze and quickly broke it. "Good."

"So plenty of time to bond with the other volunteers? Make new friends?"

She reached for her glass of water and took several sips.

"Mia?"

"We're not having wine?"

"No, I have plans for you."

She swallowed hard. "Everyone's very nice there. Rebecca's patient with the patrons. Leo doesn't have to stay all the time. I'm quite safe, Cameron."

"It's best he stays close. Just in case."

"I don't like to waste his time."

"His time is my time."

"I can handle myself."

"Don't question me again. Understand?"

Her shoulders slumped. "Perhaps you'd like to work a shift with me one day? If you have time?"

"And spoil your fun?"

"It would be nice having you there."

"Sounds like a young crowd."

"If I'm going to be running your charities—"

"Not quite sure you're ready for that just yet."

"Why not?"

"Charlie's will be undergoing some changes. I need to oversee those myself."

"What kind?"

"The details remain under wraps for now."

"You can't share them with me?"

"Why would I?"

"I wish you'd told her no."

"Who?"

"Zie. I wish you'd told her you wouldn't have a session with her. She made you sad."

"What you're seeing here, Mia, is quiet fury."

"I'm sorry she made you feel like this. I like it when you smile. You have a nice smile."

This ache was going to remain lodged in my chest permanently.

Ironic that I'd always had a thing for pain and was now going to die from it. My hand caressed my chest to soothe the agony.

"Can I get you anything?" she said.

My beautiful Mia. Could she really have fallen for another? A mystery man who'd captured her attention. Zie was right about Mia's mood. She was quieter, unsettled even, and more nervous than usual.

Though my mood was worse.

"I'm sorry," I said. "Forgive me. I have a lot on my mind."

"Of course. Let me know if there's anything I can do."

"Let me order you something else."

"I'm not really hungry. I'll have it later."

"Go put your collar on."

Her finger traced the edge of the table.

"Mia, now please."

She swallowed hard and broke my gaze. "I can't remember where I put it."

I pushed myself to my feet, rounded the table, and neared her. "Is this you rebelling?"

"No, sir."

I nudged a strand of hair behind her ear. "Make sure you wear it tomorrow."

"I lost it."

"What? When?"

"This morning. I was waiting to tell you."

A jolt of disbelief stunned me into silence.

Her hands shook. "I'm sorry. Really I am."

I was losing my submissive. Her refusal to wear my collar was the beginning of the end.

No, this wasn't happening.

"When did you last have it on?" I kept my tone calm.

"This morning, I think."

"You wouldn't be so careless…"

Her dilated pupils revealed a lie.

"I'm sorry, Cameron." Tears stung her eyes.

"Have you searched the bedroom?"

"Yes."

"Perhaps the staff—"

"No. It wasn't them."

"I meant they could've put it somewhere safe. All my staff are trustworthy."

"I lost it this morning before they came back."

I balled my hands into fists. "This is most inconvenient."

Mia trembled, and it was hard to tell if she sensed I was onto her. I shoved her plate up the table, along with her glass, and it flew off, splintering into a thousand pieces, shattering on the floor.

I grabbed her by the shoulders, lifted her up, and bent her forward over the table, bringing her wrists together behind her lower back and holding her down. Reaching over, I tugged her skirt up and her panties down.

A knock at the door.

"Not now," I shouted.

And waited for Lincoln to leave.

"Ms. Lauren, do you deserve this?" I seethed.

"Sir," she said breathlessly. "Perhaps we can talk about it—"

I slapped her ass hard. "We are."

My palm met her cheeks at a rapid pace. Mia whimpered and flinched forward. After repositioning her, I began again.

The doorbell rang.

The front door unlocked and opened.

With his booming voice, Lincoln greeted Shay, and it echoed through the foyer as he entered. Shay's cheeriness mismatched with the doom in here.

I continued to spank Mia's ass and settled into a fast rhythm, leaving bright red welts covering her cheeks.

"I'm sorry, sir."

Another knock at the door.

"Not now," I snapped.

"It's me, Cameron." It was Shay.

"You can come in," I said, and slammed Mia back down when she tried to rise.

"Please, sir," she begged.

Shay closed the door behind him and came closer.

I hitched Mia's skirt higher to reveal more of her. "Perfect timing, Mr. Gardner. We were just discussing Mia's disobedience."

He leaned back against the wall and folded his arms across his chest, ready to enjoy his vantage point.

Delivering more spanks, I felt Mia quiver beneath each strike. She'd squeezed her eyes shut, her body rigid and resisting her punishment. My palm stung, and the sound grew so loud there was no doubt the staff would hear. I grabbed a butt cheek and squeezed it, considering fucking her in front of Shay.

"Sir," she sobbed.

I lifted her up and off the table and had her stand before me. "I'm sure that will provide motivation for you to find your collar, Ms. Lauren, don't you?"

She swiped away a tear. "I'll try."

"You will find it. There will be consequences if you don't."

Her cheeks flushed brightly as she glanced over at Shay.

He offered her a sympathetic smile.

Self-hatred welled in my gut and I pulled Mia into a hug. "Do you no longer want to wear my collar, Mia?"

No longer want to be mine?

Her body crumbled against mine. "I do, sir, more than anything."

A sense of relief was still out of reach.

"Where's the contract you signed?" I said.

She peered up. "On your desk, sir. In your office."

I'd just handed Mia and her new lover twenty-million dollars to go have a new life together. Caressing my chest, this ache grew so intense I couldn't catch my breath.

Mia blinked up at me. "You still love her?"

"McKenzie? No, Mia, I don't."

She glanced coyly at Shay again.

"It's time for your lesson, Mia," I said.

She looked uncertain.

"Fencing," I said. "Despite your insolence, I'm feeling merciful."

Her face brightened slightly and she wrapped her arms around me in a hug. "I'll try to please you. I will."

I let Shay take her by the hand and lead the way out of the dining room, across the foyer, and all the way toward the gym.

I followed from a distance.

The chill of the air-conditioning hit us when we entered the large hall. The wooden floorboards were recently polished. This room was solely used for fencing.

I held back, preferring to stand by and study Mia's interaction with Shay and watch for any signs of flirting, any indication I'd been so far gone I'd not seen who she really was.

It didn't take him long to change Mia out of her dress and into the brand new fencing suit I'd had tailored for her. Shay handed Mia her new mask.

She threw me a nervous smile.

I wasn't in the mood to offer one back. I merely glared at her, wanting to see that usual effect I had on her when my control was in full force. She bit her lip, her eyes darting to Shay and back to me in nervousness.

I was a monster when I was in this mood. My cock hardened when I thought of what I would do to her later.

Shay went over the basics.

"Mia, tie your hair back," I told her.

She obediently twisted her hair into a ponytail and tied it in on itself.

I stepped forward and, with a fingertip, traced the line of a fine abrasion on the nape of her neck. "What happened here?"

She broke my gaze. "My collar caught when it came off."

"We'll replace the catch." I caressed my thumb over it. "Be more careful."

"Yes, sir," she whispered it.

My fake enthusiasm faded as I made my way out toward the office.

There on my desk lay the sealed envelope Mia had slid the contract in. Despite being tempted to shred it, I needed to know Mia was going to be taken care of.

Even if we ended in the worst kind of way.

Had ended...

I folded it over and stuck it in my jacket pocket.

Caressing my brow, I ran over Zie's scathing words about Mia, and I let out a slow protracted moan. Could I ever let Mia go? Would I become a haunting presence in her life, unable to admit I'd lost her to a younger man? He'd never feel the same way about her. I knew that with every cell of my being. He couldn't give her the kind of love she deserved. Wouldn't appreciate what he had.

Away from me, I couldn't protect her, couldn't prevent the world from getting to her.

I took a seat at my desk and swiveled in the chair, unable to remain still.

I made the call to Charlie's.

"Rebecca please," I said, and waited for the caller on the other end to go find her.

The on hold music made my blood boil. We were going to have to change that.

A click on the line.

"What's up, Dr. Cole?" answered Rebecca cheerfully.

"All good here. How's the kitchen?"

"Great. Mia's settling in. She seems to be enjoying herself."

I stopped mid-swivel and stared at my screen. "I need you to email me a list of all staff and volunteers. Addresses. Phone numbers. HR profiles."

"Sure. Is everything okay?"

"Yes."

"How does tomorrow sound?"

"Now, please."

"Yes, right away, Dr. Cole. You sure everything's okay?"

"Without delay. Understand?"

I killed the call and waited for her email.

CHAPTER 21

MY PHONE BUZZED in my pocket.

I pulled it out, shut it down, and slammed it in the desk.

Rebecca's email still hadn't come through.

The walls of my office closed in. Dark wooden panels and wall to wall books had seemed such a good idea when Terrance had first revealed his design. Now however, it made the room smaller.

Suffocating.

Over there, behind that glass cabinet, was the margarita cup, and beside it the mug Mia and I had painted during a date at Pottery Play. Afterward they'd been fired in a kiln to immortalize our chosen pieces. That spontaneous day Mia arranged had thrown me off center, bringing out a playfulness in me I'd never explored. It left the memory of an adorable date and time spent with Mia forever cherished.

Was I destined to smash them both? After love had evaporated from this place.

Loneliness seeped back to nestle in every corner.

With several clicks, I opened the tracking software on my desktop and waited for the map to appear. The red dot of the global positioning system circled on the center screen, doing its thing, waiting to pick up the tracker in Mia's collar. We'd find it in plain sight. One of the bathrooms probably.

This was out of character for Mia. Perhaps I'd been wrong

about her. Blinded by love like the idiot I'd been lately.

My spiraling thoughts needed to be reined in.

I refused to believe my doubt.

I knew Mia better than I knew myself. Something else had to be going on, and to prove it the fine hairs prickled on my forearms.

I shrank the GPS screen to the left hand corner. And refreshed my email.

A wave of uncertainty swept over me and I considered going to check on Mia and Shay. I'd left an ex-navy SEAL with the body of a rock god and the charisma to match alone with my girlfriend, a woman whose beauty made men speechless. Was I really this arrogant to believe there'd be no sparks? There'd been no sign of chemistry between them other than friendship, but I'd not been looking for any sign of betrayal.

It wouldn't be the first time Shay had taken the hand of my submissive and led her off. We had an understanding. A mutual respect. Permission had to be granted before a sub was shared.

God, now I knew how Richard felt.

Just days after I'd matched Richard and Mia together, I'd been filled with the kind of regret that could eat a man alive.

Was this a fucked up karma of my own making?

My fingers twitched for my phone and I considered calling Richard and admitting again I'd been an ass and beg him to forgive me. Go over every last detail of why Mia had to be with me. Why I was the only man who knew how to handle her, *love her.*

Zie had gone right for my jugular.

I was bleeding out.

I wasn't accustomed to this strain of jealousy. I'd left Laura's office in a quiet rage. I had to pull back on this suspicion and give Mia the benefit of the doubt.

The phone on my desk rang and I sent the call to voicemail. I wasn't on Cedars schedule tonight and Dominic could handle Chrysalis. Everyone else could go to hell.

Rebecca's email appeared and I sprang into action.

The list was long. Twenty full-time staff. Forty volunteers. None of them I'd personally hired because micromanaging wasn't my thing. Though control was, and I regretted not applying my usual brand of scrutiny to those who'd been hired at Charlie's. Evidently a chink in my armor.

Disregarding the female names, I concentrated on the men, separating them by age, and going further into their files to check for their assigned vehicle parking passes.

A red flashing in the left upper corner stole my attention and I opened the GPS back to full screen. Mia's collar was at an address in Downtown L.A.

Wait.

Think.

Mia hadn't been out of Leo's sight and Shay's men had tracked her every move before and after that. What the hell was her collar doing in L.A.?

That abrasion on her neck...

Sensing danger before I knew for certain, I went back to the previous screen. Only two volunteers had registered motorbikes.

My throat tightened when I saw the first name: *Decker Hern.*

Half in a daze, I pushed myself to my feet and hurried over to the wall, lifted off the painting, and went for the safe. After I punched in the combination, I yanked it open.

I fingered through the files and removed the one on Mia. The documentation my friend and D.A. Ethan Neilson and I had gathered and correlated to analyze the series of events on the morning of Mia's mother's death. Our investigation had been substantial and quite an achievement, bearing in mind the data went all the way back to when Mia was fourteen and lived in Charlotte.

Flicking through the files, I nudged Mia's school records aside, along with the envelope containing the forensic evidence, along with Mia's medical records obtained from her visit to the ER after they'd taken her mother to the morgue. Mrs. Lauren had been pronounced dead at the scene of their family home. We'd even obtained Mia's blood work. Rummaging through, I pulled out the police report containing the name of her mother's friend, AKA drug dealer, that Mia had provided. Adrian Herron. The man who'd quieted a fourteen-year-old Mia, when she'd hidden in the bathroom, by shooting her up with cocaine. He'd then gone on to administer the fatal dose of crack to her mom. A drug pusher's miscalculation no doubt, but no less sinister. Adrian had fled the scene and, despite assigning a private investigator on him, Herron had disappeared off the face of the earth.

Until now.

Had it been him that Mia had seen the day we'd shopped on Rodeo Drive?

With my background search software opened up, I entered Decker's name and date of birth. Decker Hern had changed his last name from Herron. He was Adrian's brother.

Damn Leo for not watching Mia's every move. She'd been out of his sight and Decker had gotten to her. Had he ripped Mia's collar off her neck this morning?

And why wouldn't she tell me if he had? Why lie?

The front door slammed.

I'd been holding my breath and couldn't remember taking my last.

I went back to checking Decker's file. An L.A. post office box came up as his address.

Fuck.

Rebecca hadn't followed protocol and gotten a home address.

A knock at the door startled me from my panicked daze.

"Hey Cam," said Shay, peeking round the door. "Sorry to interrupt. Can I come in?"

"Sure. How did Mia do?"

"Not bad. Not bad at all actually."

Shay had changed out of his fencing gear and was back in his jeans and shirt.

"That was quick," I said.

"I'm sorry. I just reacted and—"

"Please tell me you didn't stab her with a saber?"

"Course not." He shook his head. "I got a text from your dad. He's trying to get hold of you."

I released the send button on my desk phone and turned my iPhone back on.

Shay ran his hand through his hair. "I chewed Mia out for losing her collar."

I pushed myself to my feet. "I'm handling it."

"I know it's none of my business. Still, she needs to be more respectful of the gifts you give her."

"I've tracked it. The collar's at some place in L.A."

"Yes. Her friend's place. Her friend borrowed it."

"Mia told you that?"

163

He gave a nod.

"He's not a friend, Shay."

"He?"

My gaze drifted to the papers strewn on my desk. I gathered them up and slid them back inside the manila folder. I headed over to the safe and secured the file back inside.

Shay came over, knelt to pick up the painting, and handed it to me. "Mia had no idea she was being tracked."

I secured the painting back on the wall and hid the safe. "Is she upset?"

"She was when she found out how much the thing's worth."

"It's insured."

"Still, I know it has sentimental value."

"We'll find it. Shay, we have a situation. We need to talk."

Tension marred his face.

The phone shattered the quiet.

I headed back to my desk and took the call. "Yes?"

"Cameron!" my dad snapped.

"Hey, Dad. Can I call you back?"

"I've been trying to get hold of you. Why's your phone off?"

"What's going on?"

"Cam. They're filing for a leveraged buyout."

"The board? Why?"

"Check the shares."

I leaned over my desk, grabbed my mouse, and punched up Cole Tea on the screen. A jolt of adrenaline spiked my veins when I saw Cole's value.

Listening to Dad's stream of words laced in fear made my mouth go dry. This wasn't like him. He laid it out simply—Cole Tea was under a hostile takeover.

"I need you and Henry on that jet now."

"I'm on my way. Call a board meeting. Sign nothing. Understand?"

I hung up.

"What's going on?" asked Shay.

"I have to go to New York." I grabbed my jacket and headed for the door.

"When?"

"Now. The jet's fueling."

"I'll drive you."

I bolted into the foyer. "Mia."

Shay followed me out. "Cam, I brought up the collar tracker on my phone for Mia and showed it to her."

"The address of where it is?"

"Yes."

"Why?" I shrugged on my jacket

"To reassure her I could find it."

"How did she react?"

"You didn't tell her it's an antique. And it once belonged to your aunt."

"Why'd you have to tell her that, Shay?"

"It just came out."

"Mia!" I called up the stairs.

"Hello, sir," said Lincoln, appearing out of nowhere. "Ms. Lauren told me she's gone to visit a friend. I was to let you know."

A jolt of panic hit me when I read Shay's face.

"She's gone to get the collar back." Shay grabbed my arm. "Cameron, you've got to get to New York. I'll go—"

"Are your men tracking her?"

He closed his eyes in dread. "Without her collar…"

I grabbed the keys to the Bugatti Veyron.

CHAPTER 22

THE BMW WAS GONE.

I tried to steady my hands long enough to get the key fob to work. I knew Mia's collar had been ripped from her neck.

Blinded by jealousy, I'd been wrong about everything.

Shay stepped out of the subterranean elevator and waved his laptop in the air to let me know he'd retrieved it from his Mercedes. My car door clicked open, which was a good thing as I'd contemplated kicking in a window.

Shay pointed to the Bugatti Veyron. "You don't want to take something less conspicuous?"

Yes, this was a beautiful car and stood out like a whore at church, but she was the fastest roadster in the world and capable of 0-253 mph in seconds.

Exactly what we needed.

"This one's fine." I climbed in.

Shay slid into the passenger seat. "You don't think I should drive?"

"I need to do something with my hands other than kill someone."

"You drive," agreed Shay. "I like the way you drive. Very smooth. Very capable."

I revved the engine and pulled out from the parking structure, up and away from the house, speeding out the driveway.

I glanced over at Shay. "Put your seatbelt on."

"What about New York?" He held his iPhone to his ear and waited for Mia to answer her cell.

I willed her to answer.

My thoughts jumped ahead to the chaos my family and our senior executives were embroiled in right now. Henry would be on the way to LAX and I knew he'd come through, knew he had what it took to prevent those corporate bastards from decimating everything my Dad had dedicated his life to building.

He needed me right now, and I cursed the Herron brothers for wedging this time between us. The thought that one of them might have touched Mia made my skin crawl.

Shay gave a shake of his head as he left a message. "Mia. Pull over. We're right behind you. We're coming to get you."

"Can you bring up the Beamer on your laptop?" I pointed to it.

"I'm on it." He balanced his computer on his lap. "Do you want me to put an APB on her?"

"No, I don't want the cops around when we get to the house."

"And why is that?"

"They're not friends, Shay. Mia wanted you to think that. She's being blackmailed. At least that's what it looks like."

"By who?"

"Adrian Herron," I said. "His brother Decker's been working at Charlie's."

"The guy who killed her mom?"

"Yes."

"How did you discover that?"

"In a roundabout way. Rebecca confirmed it when she sent me the list of current hires."

He closed his eyes and pinched the bridge of his nose, devastated.

"It's not your fault," I said. "It's mine."

"I'm your head of security, for God's sake."

"They saw a breech and took advantage."

"You think they're blackmailing Mia? What could they possibly have on her?"

"I'm sure her family history," I said. "Knowing Mia, she's been trying to handle it herself."

"They must have seen a photo of you both together. Saw an opportunity." He shook his head. "They probably asked for money from Mia with the promise of leaving you both alone after she paid up."

"That abrasion on her neck..." I couldn't say it.

He flinched. "The bastard took her collar by force."

And I'd spanked her as a punishment and she'd still stayed quiet. Doing everything in her power to protect me, even from myself. She took that punishment I'd bestowed with an unmatched bravery.

I'd committed a monstrous act.

Self-hate welled in my gut.

Turning the corner, I sped up the driveway onto the 2.

"Mia has no idea these kind of bastards don't go away," I said. "They just keep upping the stakes."

The freeway was wide open at least.

"I've got her." He traced his finger on the screen. "She's still on the 2 and twenty miles ahead."

I shook my head to focus. "Once she's out the car..."

"We won't lose her."

Navigating around the other vehicles, I sped over to the fast lane, averting my gaze from the glare of oncoming traffic from the other side of the freeway.

"What about your flight?" he said.

"I'm going to get my girl back. And then I'm going to drop a psychological nuclear bomb on those fuckers."

"Who? The board or the Herron brothers?"

I clenched the steering wheel. "Both."

The force of opening up the Bugatti to full speed propelled us back in our seats.

Mia was more than my lover, she was my life, and I was willing to do anything to save her.

Anything.

ABOUT THE AUTHOR

Vanessa Fewings is the award-winning author of the Enthrall Sessions.

Vanessa is also the author of The Stone Masters Vampire Series, a paranormal saga.

Her romantic comedy, Piper Day's Ultimate Guide to Avoiding George Clooney, has already garnered a buzz of excitement from readers around the world. Prior to publishing, Vanessa worked as a registered nurse and midwife. She holds a Masters Degree in Psychology. She has traveled extensively throughout the world and has lived in Germany, Hong Kong, and Cyprus.

Born and raised in England, Vanessa now proudly calls herself an American and resides in California with her husband.

Next...

Cameron's Contract

Also available:

Enthrall
Enthrall Her
Enthrall Him

11856949R00104

Printed in Great Britain
by Amazon.co.uk, Ltd.,
Marston Gate.